The Vulci Damnation

by

Michael Davies

The Vulci Damnation

For information address
michaelxdavies@gmail.com

First Printing 2025

ISBN: 978-0-6454434-6-2

Other Works by Michael Davies

The Nightmares of God
The Janus Conspiracy
Accounts of a Killing
A Friendly Killing
Dreamkill
Ready, Steady, KILL!
Helix Dreams
Helix – The Second Renaissance
Helix-Ascension
The Ninth of the Month Murders
The Death Gambit
The Internet Murders
The Moriarty Awards

For the Young Adults (12-18)
The Many Worlds of Mickie Dalton
The Many Galaxies of Mickie Dalton
The Many Universes of Mickie Dalton
The Strange World of Mark and Anna

For the 8-12 age group
The Julie Malloy Gang and the Smugglers
The Quest for the Locket
The Secret of Yuri Kirilenko
The United Nations and the Extra-Terrestrial
The Secret of Charlotte's Cello
The Star of the Yshan Kings
The War of the Yshan Empire
The Star of the New Yshan Empire
The Red Fog of Time
The Mysterious Recorder and The Door to Elsewhere
Prisoners of the Picture
A Step Back in Time
What Can't be Seen Can Exist
How I Spent My Evening

For the Little Ones (3-5)
Mary's World

Acknowledgements

This is the sixth book written in collaboration with Greg Dickson. Instead of our standard approach of a series of three-day, intensive brainstorming sessions at my home over several months, this time I sent Greg each new day's production for later discussion and review by telephone. Most days, this involved anything from five hundred words to over 2000.

Yet again, it seems to have worked.

My thanks to Greg.

And to Jacqui Wynn, great thanks for her professional and knowledgeable review, making this a much better story than it had been

Chapter 1 – The Present Day

"This is amazing, Dad," said thirteen-year-old Lisa. She was totally thrilled to have accompanied her father and been allowed to come with him into this massive structure where several of her father's students were working. "I've heard you talk about the Etruscans a lot and they sounded so weird. So who were they? Where did they come from?"

Kendricks laughed. "Those questions have taken up the last twenty years of my life!" he replied. "They may be the most extraordinary civilisation in the whole world, and people have been studying them for centuries. There's an awful lot we still don't know about them. Let's start with what we do know. They'd been a civilisation for at least nine hundred years in what we call BCE, Before the Common Era, or what used to be called BC. Exactly where they came from is still an argument among historians and archaeologists, but I incline to the theory that they originated in what is now Turkey."

"And they moved here when?" asked Lisa.

"We know they were here in Northern Italy for at least a thousand years up until they faded out under Roman influence, two or three centuries BCE."

Professor Robert Kendricks was in his element. He was at the head of a highly qualified and expert archaeological team, in the area that had made his global reputation, and he had his daughter with him, his only child and the light of his life.

"I'm glad I could come with you, Dad," said Lisa, clinging to her father's arm as they moved along. "I didn't want to go shopping with Mum, she's so bad-tempered, always finds something to get angry about with me."

"I'm glad, too. But we have to treat your mother carefully," said Kendricks. "I think she has problems at work and her home life as a child was pretty rough. Let's not talk about her."

He gently stroked Lisa's hair. "Let's concentrate on this amazing place. We're in an incredible tomb, possibly the finest example of the Etruscan civilisation."

"Did they all get buried in the same place?" Lisa felt fascinated by this whole experience, possibly because she was able to share it with her father.

"Only the great families did that," replied Kendricks. He stopped before one of the larger paintings.

"This appears to be a family portrait," he said. "This is the tomb of what was known to be the Vulci Family, one of twelve great families that ruled the Etruscans, or the Rasenna as they called themselves. Our historians have studied it intensely and they believe there are three siblings, an older brother, a younger one and a sister. The younger one is the one holding a sword, and there appears to be anger in his stance and expression. We don't know any more than that."

* * *

478 BCE – the Peak of the Etruscan Era

"Those damned Tarquinia dogs have killed Velthur." Sethre Vulci was in a furious rage, holding his sword as if he was about to behead the servant who had brought him the news. "He was our cousin, he was the best of the Vulci family." The rage showed in his red face, above the heavy beard and the startling blue eyes that were wide open, showing the whites.

"This cannot be tolerated." Sethre's brother, Aranthur was calmer, but the anger still showed in the tension of his body and the way his fingers tapped on the hilt of his sword in the scabbard at his side. "It's time we showed the Tarquinia that this war will be stopped with their destruction."

"Can we get some of the other tribes to declare war on them, do you think?" Sethre had calmed down a little, but his grip on his sword was still tight.

"I doubt it, my brother," replied Aranthur. "Our people have survived and prospered for centuries without internal strife. Already, many of the leaders of the Rasenna league of Twelve Families have expressed dismay at the feud between us and the Tarquinia. Both of us have killed family members of both tribes and can we remember why it started? We cannot. I see no value in continuing the killing."

"Those are the first sensible words I have heard from you," said a strong, baritone voice from the doorway.

The siblings turned to face their father as he walked into the room. He was a man in his seventies, but stood straight, his shoulders back and his snow-white hair framed a strong face with a straight nose, a wide mouth usually set in a smile. Today, he was frowning.

"As my son said, this killing is simply madness, it has no purpose and must stop," he continued.

All three of his children showed the respect they had for their father. It was deserved. Caeles had been a major figure in the leadership of the Rasenna for many years, highly influential in consolidating the strength of the Twelve Families.

"I have been trying to tell these lunatics that for years," said Hathri, the youngest sibling and the only girl. She had stayed silent while the two men let out their anger, but her own irritation had shown.

Caeles smiled fondly at his daughter.

"Both of them would rather swing a sword than engage in conversation," he said. "But I'm delighted that you can see sense, even if they can't."

"So what must we do, Father?" asked Sethre after directing an angry glare at Hathri.

"First, put your sword down," said Caeles with a smile. "Unless you want to fight me, perhaps?"

All three siblings laughed. Caeles had been a notable warrior for almost all his life, responsible for the deaths of many enemies and always seen at the head of troops when battle commenced.

"No Father, I have no wish to fight you," said Sethre.

Caeles nodded. "In three weeks, the Fanum Voltumnae will meet. This is the best time to raise issues, and I am sure the Speaker will raise this one. I will not be there, so Sethre, Aranthur, you must speak for the Vulci. The Families have always condemned this feud, they will do again, you must be prepared to agree to end the killing."

Finally, Sethre sheathed his sword and walked to the table to pour himself a glass of wine.

"Then there has to be another way," he said. "The Tarquinia do not deserve to live. Could we talk to the Romans? They seem to be growing in power, and I worry that they may take over this land and rule it with their own gods and their own laws. Maybe we can persuade them that the Tarquinia are a threat to their future?"

"That may be one approach," said Caeles. "I urge you to think about a way that does not involve the killing of anyone. If our family wishes to lead the Rasenna in the future, we must be seen as wise, competent and not violent. Can you do that?"

Sethre bowed his head. "We will do that, Father," he said. "Aranthur and I, we will discuss this."

"I am pleased," said Caeles. "Now, I am an old man and I must retire back to my room. I shall tell Calaina what you have told me."

"Please tell our mother we will follow your advice as we always have," said Aranthur.

All three siblings bowed their heads as their father left. Sethre finally lifted the wineglass he had filled when his father had entered and took a deep draught.

Aranthur joined him and drank his wine in thoughtful silence. After a few minutes, he broke his silence.

"The Romans are certainly a problem," he said, "and I doubt we have more than a few years before they challenge us for these lands. We may need all the forces of the Rasenna to keep them away. But as for the Tarquinia? Let me try my usual approach. Give me a week, I will kill a Tarquinian, and nobody will be able to claim I or any other Vulci is responsible."

"You just promised our father that you will do no such thing," said Hathri. Her anger showed clearly in her clenched fists and rigid stance. "Will you break your vow immediately?"

"Despite what Father said, there may be no alternative," said Aranthur.

Sethre needed no time for review. "Do it," he said.

"Wait, please," called Hathri. Still only sixteen, but beginning to show the extraordinary beauty for which the Vulci women were renowned. "That only prolongs the war. Aranthur will kill a Tarquinian, the Tarquinia will vow vengeance, and they will kill another of our family. It gains us nothing. Our father is a wise man, and we must obey him."

Aranthur displayed irritation at being questioned, but soon he calmed down.

"I have a better way," he said. "Perhaps we can damn those animals into future death where the world has no Tarquinia in it."

"Tell me more," said Sethre. Aranthur's words had calmed him down considerably with the thought that there could be a solution to this crisis.

"Let us call in Larce, the priest. He has been with our family for many years. I believe I have a suggestion."

"You are my brother. I have always valued your counsel," said Sethre.

"Will you fools never give up waving your swords around like some other part of your body?" said Hathri, contempt in every word.

The men ignored her.

*   *   *

"This feud between your families has always caused concern among our people," said Larce the priest. He was an elderly man, straight in body and with a face that reflected wisdom and kindness. He had been the family priest for many years and was regarded as a friend and counsellor by the siblings who had known him since their earliest days. "The reasons for it have been lost in time, so any way of reducing the killings will be seen with favour by the Twelve Families."

"This is what the Vulci family asks of you," said Aranthur. Carefully, he described the work he wished the priest to accomplish. When he had finished, the priest nodded.

"The Twelve Families who lead the Rasenna have been the powerful force keeping the peace and the wealth of the region since they formed the League of Twelve over a century ago. The Tarquinia are often seen as the weak point in the League and their end will be seen as valuable to all of them. As a priest of the true gods, I cannot do your bidding, but I will have it done."

"How will you do that?" Sethre showed great curiosity.

"It cannot be a priest of the Rasenna that does it. The Twelve Families have always worshipped the true gods and a priest of those cannot do what you are requesting. I will call an alternative."

"Do you know of someone who can do this?" asked Aranthur. Sethre's curiosity was matched by his brother.

"It frightens me that I do," replied the priest. "It frightens me even more that the process will be initiated. It goes against all my beliefs and commitment to the Gods of the Twelve Families. But I will arrange it, though I will not be here when the task is begun."

"How long?" asked Sethre.

"Give me two days. Someone will come here."

"Agreed," said Sethre.

The Present Day – The Tomb of the Sun and the Moon

"This picture is a puzzle," said Professor Kendricks as he and Lisa stood near the wall looking at the faded painting. Around them, the slow work and soft conversations of others of the archaeology team continued. "We think it's a group meeting of some sort, but it's seriously faded, though we can identify three male figures. Oddly enough, there's a similar painting in one of the other tombs, which we believe is owned by another of the Twelve Families, the Tarquinia. We had a specialist examine both of them and we photographed them so he could apply some very advanced techniques to improve the clarity, and he should be about ready.. ah! Here is the first one, the work he has done on this painting here. Let's see what we have."

He looked down at his open laptop computer, the screen now filled with the same image as on the wall in front of them, but with brighter colours and sharper edges The three figures standing now had much clearer faces.

"Well, look at that," exclaimed Kendricks. "That man with the sword is the same one as in the previous picture, which we assumed was a Vulci family group. There's no indication of who the other two are, but it looks like this is some sort of gathering. I'd hazard a fairly educated guess that this is a meeting of the Twelve Families."

His laptop pinged again and a second picture appeared. Kendricks studied it for a few moments then lowered it for Lisa to see.

"It's almost the same scene," he said. "There's a gathering of some sort, there's a man with a sword, but his face is not as clear as in the first one. But I think we can assume it's the same Vulci person. The second man has a much clearer face. This picture came from the Tarquinia family tomb, so it's probable that he's of that family. The third man is not clear, the artist has not made any attempt to show his face clearly, but he's standing some way apart from the rest of the gathering, and he seems unusually tall. Maybe he's the speaker or chairman or equivalent. This is fascinating."

He closed down his laptop. "I wish we understood more of what that meeting was all about. It would throw more light on this whole civilisation, of which we know next to nothing. Let's go and see how the others are progressing."

* * *

478 BCE, The City of Volsinii, Etruria

"The League of Twelve will begin the Fanum Voltumnae, our annual session," said Thresu of the City of Vetalonia. He was an imposing man, a full two metres tall and muscular in build, renowned as a warrior, a man few could stand against and succeed.

The room filled with representatives of the twelve families became quiet, even the angry words being exchanged between the two feuding families went silent. This annual gathering of the *de facto* government of the Etruscan people was the biggest event of the League and held great power.

"There are many things to debate this year," continued Thresu, the declared chairman for the gathering. "But the most critical is the ongoing warfare between the families of Tarquinia and Vulci. It is threatening our nation's security and weakens us as the Roman forces grow in power. Too many of us have died in this ugliness."

He faced the Vulci group of the two brothers and the supporting trio of other family members. "I see that my old friend Caeles is not with you. We are the poorer for his absence. Sethre, Aranthur, do you speak for your father?"

"The Tarquinia began this war when they seized many of our Vulci lands," said Sethre Vulci from the floor. "We have only tried to reclaim what is ours."

"It was never yours," shouted Ramtha Tarquinia. "The Tarquinia families lived in those lands for centuries before the Vulci invaded and stole them, killing many of our people."

"That is enough," bellowed Thresu. "This will stop now. It seems that you do indeed lack your father's wisdom."

The room fell silent, but the anger in the two opponents almost radiated from them and threatened to erupt in violence at any moment. Thresu directed his powerful glare at both for a full minute until they subsided, as all men did before Thresu.

"Sethre Vulci, as the leader of your family, will you declare here and now that there will be no more killings of Tarquinia?"

Sethre looked briefly at his brother Aranthur, standing beside him, then looked back at the chairman. "I do so declare." The tension in having to speak the words made his voice harsh.

"And you, Ramtha, as the leader of the Tarquinia family, will you also declare that there will be no more killings of Vulci?"

Ramtha was silent for a moment, then spoke reluctantly.

"I so declare."

"Then the matter is ended," said Thresu.

He was wrong.

"The Vulci will kill you pigs no more," shouted Sethre. "But I call upon the Gods to punish the Tarquinia for their crimes."

"You may call upon the Gods all you want," responded Ramtha. "They will not obey you. You will find that those calls will be taken up by the Devil and his demons and they will make you pay for your insolence."

"That is enough," shouted Thresu. "The League has far more critical matters to deal with than the childish battles of immature children. Now stay silent or leave the building and perhaps leave the League as well. We have no use for this."

In the face of the growing hostility from the other ten family leaders, Sethre and Ramtha subsided.

"We have agreed to cease the killings," said Sethre. "But in no way does that prevent the hatred, and we must have our revenge for the evils done to our family."

"You said you had an idea about that, the last time we met," said Aranthur. "You suggested we may have a curse placed by the Gods on those Tarquinia. We even talked to our priest, the man who has advised and guided this family for decades. Tell us more, brother."

"Yes, we talked to the priest, Larce. You may recall, he said it was not a thing he could do, being a faithful servant of the True Gods. But he knew somebody who could."

"Then I think it is time we told the priest to call for that service."

"I agree," said Aranthur.

* * *

The Priest, Larce, stopped at the entrance to the old house on the outskirts of the town. Even there, he felt the temperature drop and sensed the presence of great evil. He had a strong urge to turn and walk away, but he had made a commitment to one of the Twelve Families of Etruria, leaders of the Rasenna for the thousands of years before and since since they had moved to this region. One did not turn away from the

Twelve Families, even if the commitment conflicted with all his beliefs. Finally, the Priest entered the building to find a large gloomy hall with a handful of men gathered in a circle around a very old man in the centre. That man was clearly the leader of this gathering. He saw Larce enter and stepped away from the circle.

Larce felt a sickening jolt in his chest. He knew this man and had done all his life.

"That will do for now, brothers," the old man said, and the men moved to one side, after giving Larce a long, hostile stare. Larce ignored it, concentrating his entire focus on the man approaching him.

"Well, Larce," said the man. "It has been many years." His voice was that of the very old, weak, rasping, barely audible.

"Those years have not treated you well," said Larce. He was struggling with the shock of meeting what had been his little brother who now looked older than his parents when they had died. There was a sour taste in his mouth.

"Perhaps not. But what I may have paid in years, I have earned much in power in this world. I have forgotten those innocent years, perhaps you with them."

"But I have never forgotten you, and how you abandoned the one true faith," said Larce. "Our parents died of shock when you walked away from the Gods and our family. What has happened to you? I was your elder brother, I cared for you as an infant and protected you. Now you look thirty years older than I am."

The old man turned an angry face to Larce. "And you thought I should be everlastingly grateful to you for your treatment of me? Let me tell you what it was like to be your younger sibling. Our parents favoured you in all things. Your birthdays were celebrated in far more generous ways than mine. Your wishes were always heeded, mine mostly ignored. That was why I turned to the Underworld gods. And I got their attention. You think our parents died of shock because I abandoned their gods? No, they died because I summoned a demon and killed them."

Larce was frozen in horror. "You summoned a demon? You were twelve years old. How could you summon a demon?"

The old man emitted a short, dry laugh of contempt.

"Anything is possible for those who try. I found the old books, I found the rituals and I practiced them. Finally, I performed them fully and a demon came to me. He did what I asked, and I have never looked back. I recognised where the power in the world lay, and I have sworn allegiance to it ever since. The Gods you continue to serve are toothless."

Larce was just able to speak. "You killed our parents? My God, how could you have been my brother? What evil was in you from the start?"

"Yes, once we were brothers," replied the man with a cold smile. "Once, we believed the same things, the same gods, the right of the Twelve Families to rule absolutely. But I grew up. I found powers greater than we knew and I wanted my share of them. The Gods of the Rasenna could never grant me those."

"How could you abandon our gods?" Larce felt a deep well of sickness in his soul and the first trickles of fear. Had he tempted evil by entering this place?

"I didn't. But there are more than gods in our world, there are also servants of the Underworld. Now I follow them. They give us more than those limited gods you still worship." He gave a sharp gesture of dismissal. "So why are you here, my one-time brother? I must say, it was a shock to see you. My followers were disturbed when you broke into our communication with the Underworld. It will take much effort on my part to keep them from making you pay for it."

"They could punish me for entering? Will I leave alive?" Larce felt the cold chill of fear run more strongly down his body. He had not anticipated this.

"Alive, yes. Damaged? Possibly. Not physically, but you may encounter some of the more malignant powers of those we worship. But as your one-time brother, I will try and prevent it. So now, what has made you risk your body and your soul by entering this temple of the Underworld?"

"I have to ask for your services, Thefarie. The Vulci family require it."

The man shook his head. "I am no longer Thefarie, that name was abandoned many years ago. Now I am Charun."

Larce took a step backward in shock. "You have taken the name of the demon of Death?"

"He guards the Underworld. He is all-powerful. I display my commitment to him by taking his name. Now, enough of this. What is this service that the Vulci require and what manner of service is it that they cannot ask their gods for it?"

Larce struggled to control himself and speak normally.

"They wish to lay a curse on their ancient enemies, the Tarquinia. Both families have sworn to the Council of Fanum Voltumnae at Volsinii that the bloodletting will end, but they have decided on this path instead."

Charun laughed, a dry, humourless sound.

"Perhaps that will end the bloodletting, but it will only direct the killing into a different path. I will do that small service, but there will be a price."

"That will be between you and the Vulci. I want no dealings there."

"No, Larce, you must stay in your vows, that is true." Charun's face retained a smile, but it reflected no warmth. Larce felt a shiver run through him again. Something evil was being created here, he knew.

"And the price will be greater than the Vulci know," added Charun. "I thank you for bringing this transaction to me."

"I will leave it in your hands," said Larce and turned away. As he walked towards the exit, Charun's frightening laugh followed him. On one side of the room, the men who had seen him enter reappeared and lined up along the path Larce had to take to the outside. Trembling, he forced himself to walk, not looking to the side at the line of cold, frightening faces. They made no gesture towards him, but he sensed their waves of hatred flooding at him.

He felt the jolt in his heart and fell to the ground, every atom of him feeling pain. Gasping for breath, he tried to crawl towards the door but couldn't move. The pain got worse, and he knew he was about to die.

A huge voice rang out through the building.

"STOP," it called. The pain stopped, but Larce was too weak to stand up. A figure appeared at his face, though Larce could only see the shoes. Then Charun bent down and helped Larce to his feet.

"That is the last time I will help you," the ancient man said. "But now you see the powers gained by worshipping the Gods of the Underworld. Now leave, brother. I will do as the Vulci ask, but they may regret it." He released Larce's arm and stood back.

Still shaking, Larce staggered to the doorway. He made it outside, but the rest of the day and well into the night, Larce spent in the temple of the Gods, praying for their protection

* * *

The Present Day – The Tomb of the Sun and the Moon

"This one has puzzled all of us," said Kendricks.

They had stopped before a second painting on the wall. It showed the same family group of the three siblings, but standing behind them was an old man, his hands raised in the air. But what was horrifying was the foreground. It showed a boy, perhaps a teenager, with blood all over his clothes.

"We think that the boy is a servant," said Kendricks. "His clothing is simple, more like a peasant, perhaps a servant to the Vulci family. But clearly, something ugly has happened. It looks like the boy has just been lethally attacked while others of the family stood without acting. That figure in the background could well be a priest. Maybe this was a blood sacrifice for something terrible."

478 BCE – the House of Vulci, Etruria

The man brought into the room by a servant looked old, so old it looked difficult for him to walk, even with the stick he used in one hand. There was no hair on his head, the face was dry and wrinkled like the desert sands after a storm and the hand that held the stick looked barely strong enough.

"I have been told what you want," said the ancient man.

"And can you do it?" Aranthur looked doubtful.

The old man stared at him, and the look was so frightening that even Aranthur, a noted warrior and killer of men took a step backward.

"Do not doubt a servant of the Underworld." The voice was like the speaker, dry, barely audible, but the eyes shone with power. "I will do as you ask, but there is a price to pay before I can start."

"What price?" asked Aranthur.

"Someone must die, here and immediately. Send for a slave."

Aranthur nodded, walked to the door and opened it, spoke a few words and returned. A few minutes passed before the door opened again and a boy walked in, looking terrified. He was perhaps fifteen.

Aranthur pointed at a spot in the middle of the room and the boy slowly walked to it. His trembles were violent, and water dropped from his body as he lost control. Aranthur gave him no time to be frightened any further. He drew his sword, moved the few paces and drove the weapon into the body of the boy. The youth screamed, clutched at his stomach as blood erupted and covered his tunic, then collapsed on the floor, his body twitching a few times, then went still.

The old man walked up to the corpse, bent his head and then began walking counterclockwise in a circle around the blood-soaked body. A sound emitted from him, a slight, wordless song of little melody that gradually grew into a strong, hypnotic call of horror. As he stopped, the body of the boy twitched, moved a little, then stood in one fluid motion and smiled at the Vulci siblings.

"I thank you for this body," he said. "That old one has become too difficult, and I can abandon it now."

As he spoke, the ancient man fell to the floor, clearly dead.

Sethre, Aranthur and Hathri were all silent, severely shocked by what had happened.

"I will need three objects which will carry the Vulci curse," said the boy. There was blood all over his tunic, on his arms and on his face, but he seemed unaffected.

"What objects?" asked Sethre, his voice trembling slightly.

The boy began to walk to the siblings. As he did, he left a trail of blood on the floor. He stopped in front of Hathri. She took a step back, her face ashen, her hands clasped tight. The boy pointed at her gold necklace.

"That," he said, his pleasant smile shocking in the bloody face.

"It was my mother's," gasped Hathri, her voice almost a whisper.

The boy said nothing but held out his hand. Tears flooded down Hathri's face as she unclasped the necklace and handed it to him. He turned away and walked up to Sethre. He pointed at the unusually large ring on Sethre's hand.

Sethre stared at it. "That is a family treasure, awarded to the one who does most to maintain the family honour. I earned it in blood and pain, fighting in Etruscan wars against its enemies."

"That," said the boy.

Accepting the inevitable, Sethre took the ring off his finger and dropped it into the boy's outstretched hand.

Aranthur visibly flinched as the boy turned to him and moved to stand facing him.

"And what do you have that will allow me to complete my task?" said the boy.

Aranthur shook his head, the fear in his face obvious.

"Only this," he said, showing the copper bracelet on his left wrist. "It is worth nothing, but I took it from the leader of the Gauls we defeated. It is a badge of honour only."

"Then that will do," said the boy and held out his hand, waiting motionless while Aranthur unclipped the bracelet and handed it over. With all three items, the boy walked to the dead body of the ancient priest. He ripped a panel of cloth from the man's tunic, knelt down and placed the necklace, the ring and the bracelet on the cloth. Still kneeling, he held his hands over the jewels. He held that pose for a few minutes, his eyes closed. Then he raised his hands, placed them together and held them over his head, looking upwards. He began to chant in a deep, musical voice. It was so different from the light voice of the dead body of the priest, that it could have been a different person

"I call on the Gods of the Rasenna, to Catha, God of the Sun, Laran, the God of War, Leinth, the Angel of Death, on Aritimi, Minrva and Pacha, to curse the family of the Tarquinia. Make these items the carrier of the curse, so that for all of time to come, any wearer of one of the Vulci bloodline will be filled with the ability to recognise any member of the Tarquinia and the need to kill them. I call on the Gods of the Underworld to make this so."

For several minutes, the boy remained silent in that pose, then he dropped his hands and turned to the others.

"The curse is laid," he said. "What you do with these pieces is now up to you."

Deeply moved, the two men bowed before him and stood silently as the boy left the house. Only the deep-throated weeping of Hathri broke the silence

"What should we do?" asked Sethre.

"We need to regain the trust of the League of Twelve," said Aranthur. "We have lost much of it, as have the Tarquinia filth with our war. Let us remove those items from the world for a long time. You should place them with your body when you die and are buried in the family Tomb of the Sun and the Moon, but leave instructions with your sons to remove them some time after your death. That way, we will not be seen as warmongers and killers, but agents of peace. What happens after your sons remove the items is up to them, but the war against the Tarquinia will continue until they have been wiped out, however far into the future, even a thousand years."

"The Gods willing I have sons in the future," said Sethre with a smile.

Aranthur reflected it. "Your marriage to Messia is set for the summer," he said. "I am sure you both know what to do."

Both men laughed and poured more wine. Hathri didn't join them in drinking.

"How do we tell our Father that we have disobeyed him?" she said, tears choking her voice.

"We haven't," replied Sethre, a smile of triumph on his lips. "We have promised that we will not personally kill any more Tarquinia. But they will still die, just not at our hands."

Hathri walked out of the room.

478 BCE, The House of Tarquinia, Etruria

Kavie Tarquinia's anger was cold, but forceful enough to have driven several of the servants out of the hall where the family seniors were gathered. They were well aware that his anger, while cold, could explode into violence at any time.

"Those damned Vulci have done as they threatened," said the scion of the family. "They have called in the priests and placed a curse on us. Does anyone know how it has been structured?"

"One of our people in their household told us that they cursed three items of jewellery, a gold necklace, a ring and a copper bracelet." Elinei Tarquinian, the eldest sister of Kavie's siblings spoke clearly, controlling her anger.

"Perhaps that shows us how to respond," said Kavie.

"Explain, dear brother," replied Elinei.

"The history of our family tells us that on two occasions, our ancestors summoned demonic forces to assist their survival. The method is described in detail."

"And you think that is the way needed now?" Vel Tarquinia was the youngest of the siblings, only in his thirties, but already the proud owner of the title of "Vulci Killer" for his murder of three members of the enemy family.

"Our way was banned in the Fanum Voltumnae in Volsinii," said Vel. "If we continue along that path, the eleven other members of the League would declare war on us. We could not withstand that."

Elinei released her anger. "Then it is time we called upon the Gods to help us."

"The Gods will not help us in destroying one of the Families," said Vel. "That is said in all our sacred writings."

"So you agree with the suggestion of summoning demonic help?" Kavie smiled at his young brother.

Vel nodded.

Kavie paused, as if gathering his thoughts for what to tell his family next.

Finally, he spoke. "Yesterday, I read the instructions for summoning a demon. I found the details written in Greek on a linen tapestry. I have no idea who wrote them, but like all of us, educated at the finest schools, I can read Greek. I was anticipating your comment. Let us meet here in two hours, and I will collect what we need."

When the others of the family returned to the meeting hall, Kavie was already at work. He had drawn a ring about three metres in diameter with red paint and placed twelve candles at equal points around it.

As the others entered, Kavie lit the candles and took his seat with his siblings a short distance from the burning circle. "A prayer was recited at each previous summoning," he said. "The language is unknown to me, but I have learnt the words. Let us begin."

He stood up and began a chant that was incomprehensible to the others. It lasted only a minute and when finished, Kavie walked round the circle in an anticlockwise direction. After three circuits, he stopped and covered his eyes. Silence reigned for several minutes, then something happened.

Kavie began to speak, but his voice had changed. It was deeper than his normal voice and carried a small echo after each word. A shiver of fear ran through the others in the room. There was huge menace in the voice.

"If you wish to summon me in the service of the family, a price must be paid," said the alien voice. "It is the same price the Vulci paid when they summoned one of us."

Only Vel Tarquinia found his voice, though it shook a little as he spoke.

"What is your price? And will you tell us who you are?"

"I am one that serves the Great One. You conducted the act of summoning, but did not provide someone who knew it, so I have taken the body of one of you for now. To complete this, your price is a fresh death. Bring someone here who can die."

Walking carefully to prevent his legs shaking so much that he would fall, Vel went to the door and called in the servant standing outside. It was a young girl. She looked frightened as she entered and stopped just inside the doorway.

"Come, child," said Vel and gently led her to stand in the circle that Kavie had painted. Small sobs came from the girl and tears ran down her cheeks. Standing behind her, Vel took a dagger from his belt without the girl seeing and slammed it into the back of her neck. She cried out in pain as Vel turned her round and thrust the blade into her chest by the heart. Blood erupted over her body as she fell to the floor, and she was dead before she was fully laid out.

"The price is paid," said Kavie in that alien voice.

The body of the dead girl twitched once, then became immobile again. A few seconds later, it twitched again, then moved with several motions before sitting up. The girl stared at the watchers, her bloody face smiling. Blood stained her garments and lay thick on her arms and legs. She slowly stood up, still staring at the group.

The fear in the watchers could be felt. Even Vel, their greatest warrior was shaking. Kavie was struggling to stay upright as his body trembled violently.

"Why have you summoned me?" the frightful, bloody corpse said. "I am grateful for the body you have supplied, but this is not easy for me. So again, why?"

"The Vulci tribe has placed a curse on my family," said Kavie.

"It cannot be lifted," said the demon.

"We know that," replied Kavie. "What we want from you is a response that will make them pay for their evil."

"The curse was placed on three items of jewellery. Together, they will make the wearers of those items desire to kill any member of the Tarquinia. But those are items that would only be worn by young women," said the demon. "I can use that fact."

"How will you do that?"

"As placed, the curse would apply to any person in the Vulci bloodline. Now I can make it that only when a female who has yet to achieve maidenhood wears any of those three items, she will be filled with a lust to kill. When she wears two of them, the lust will grow such as to become irresistible. The third item will direct that lust to any descendant of the Vulci tribe for all time into the future and give her the ability to recognise the ancestry of Tarquinia. Once she has it, she will have it for all time."

"Only young women?"

"That is the force. No others will be affected, whether they wear those pieces or not."

Kavie struggled to hide the trembles and tightness in his throat. "But what price did the Vulci pay for this curse?"

The bloodied corpse laughed, a chilling sound.

"They will live in fear, all of them, for all their lives, that I will demand greater payment. But they don't realise that my payment is the deaths of the Tarquinia who will die at Vulci hands. But now I will pay you my reward for summoning me and giving me some time in a human body again. I treasure such moments."

"How can we reward you?" Kavie. His fear had partially subsided, but tremors still shook him, and he found it difficult to look at the demon.

"Not you. The Vulci will pay my price. For every Tarquinia killed under this curse, two Vulci will also die. That remains my price for all of time."

"That is acceptable." Kavie spoke with greater ease.

"Then I will leave you. I wish to enjoy this body you have given me."

The girl's mutilated body left the ring and walked out of the room, trailing a line of blood. A gust of icy wind blew through the room and snuffed out the candles around the ring. Elinei broke into terrified weeping.

"What have we done?" she said through her hands covering her face. "By all the gods, what have we done?"

Nobody could answer.

* * *

"I have been thinking." Kavie had asked his siblings to meet in the private room that the Tarquinia family leaders used for their relaxation and comfort. Luxurious, deep cushions ringed the room, Beautiful wall hangings covered almost every inch of the surrounds, and a small table held flagons of different wines and glasses.

The other two looked at him, not bothering to ask the obvious question.

"Remember what the demon told us about the Vulci curse that has been laid on this family," continued Kavie. "He told us that there were three items that had been made the instruments of the curse. Each item, a necklace, a ring and a bracelet would, when all worn by a female, allow the wearer to recognise a Tarquinian and be driven to kill him or her."

"But only one would cause a lust to kill, and two items would make that lust powerful," agreed Elinei. "Only when all three items are worn, will the wearer identify Tarquinia. Where is this taking you, my brother?"

"A powerful place, dear sister. Surely this means that if we can keep at least one of those three permanently out of the Vulci possession, then never could a woman, even wearing two of the items, recognise a Tarquinian and be able to kill them."

Elinei took a deep swallow of the wine glass and stared at Kavie.

"You may just have saved the family from a dreadful crime, dear brother," she said. "So now we must discuss how to gain possession of one of those cursed pieces."

"We have two of our people working unknown in the Vulci nest of rats," said Vel, standing by the table and pouring himself a glass of wine. "They have been there for two years, they are accepted by the Vulci as faithful servants. We pay them well to maintain this pretence, so they get double the salary that the other servants receive."

"An excellent deal for them," said Elinei. "And so far, they have done nothing to merit that affluence."

"Not quite," said Kavie. "Once a month, they meet secretly with one of my servants and tell him what has happened in the Vulci house. That is a dangerous act, if it became known, they would be killed in a very ugly way. But it's how we learnt of the curse and that was critical for us."

"Agreed," said Elinei. "So now instruct your servant that the next time they meet, the Vulci servant must somehow access the cursed items and take one of them."

"Some part of that we already know," said Kavie. "Our agent has done well. She knows that the smallest item is the ring worn by Sethre Vulci for his wartime exploits. I know that ring, I have seen it many times. We can make up a copy and when our agent is able, she can substitute our copy for the one cursed by the demon. The Vulci will never know, and their curse will never take effect."

"And once we have that ring, it must be buried with you in your tomb when you die," said Elinei. "That will ensure the curse is dead. Instruct your servant, Kavie."

"This we must drink to," said Kavie.

* * *

472 BCE, The Vulci Tomb of the Sun and the Moon, Etruria

Aranthur Vulci had tears running down his cheeks.

"My brother was one of the greatest men who ever lived," he said, struggling to keep his voice under control. "His death tears a great hole in the Vulci Family. But this Family has been a major leader of the Etruscan people for many hundreds of years, and we shall continue to be one of the strongest pillars of the League of Twelve. I pray that his tomb will remain sacrosanct through all of time."

His sister, Hathri held out a box made of beautifully polished cedar.

"I had our best craftsman make this," she said. Her voice was calm, but under the dark veil of mourning, her eyes were red from weeping. "It contains the three items cursed by the demon those years ago. I know that you also instructed the builders of Sethre's tomb to create a hidden, secret space to contain this box, so that it may never be found until the servants of the Great One are ready for the curse to be activated again."

She opened the box and she and Aranthur took a last look at the gold necklace, the ring and the copper bracelet. Aranthur took it, closed the lid and moved to a spot along one wall. Marked only by a tiny dot, the presence of anything behind was quite unnoticeable. Aranthur pushed on the dot, a small opening appeared, and he placed the box inside the space revealed. The gap closed, Aranthur wiped the dot clean and stood back.

"Now it is up to the Great One," he said, and the brother and sister left the tomb.

Chapter 2

The Vulci Tomb of the Sun and the Moon

The archaeological team of the university, led by the head of the department, Professor Robert Kendricks was hard at work. This was the third expedition and after two weeks, the collection of artworks, finery, jewellery and engraved writing on various slabs of stone had slowed to a trickle. The linguists were intensely engaged in trying to translate the Etruscan writings, something that was considered as difficult as Egyptian hieroglyphics before the discovery of the Rosetta Stone, but so far, no such breakthrough had occurred, and the linguists were making slow progress.

Kendricks knew the expedition was winding down as he wrote his notes on the day's work. As he switched off his laptop, an odd sensation gripped him. There was something to be done, something to be found. For a moment, he worried that perhaps the workload, or the closed atmosphere had affected him, and he sat back and tried to take deep breaths. Nothing worked. Finally, he gave up and got to his feet, intending to go outside and get fresh air.

As he passed the tomb of what was known to be of a high-ranking Vulci family member, the strange urge got stronger. Submitting to whatever subconscious thought was gripping him, he turned into the tomb. The feeling became even more powerful.

"This is weird," he muttered and looked round the room. Something forced him to study a section of wall. Giving up on fighting the strange effect, he moved to the wall and touched a small area without understanding just what had made him do that. To his astonishment, a small section of the wall lifted outward, revealing a space behind. In utter fascination, Kendricks saw a wooden box, the wood glowing as if freshly oiled and polished. He extracted the box and studied it, almost hypnotised by what was happening. After a few moments, he opened it. There were three items lying on soft cloth, a gold necklace that Kendrick realised from his experience, was worth at least a hundred thousand pounds. The middle item was a ring, something he recognised as a symbol of valour, given to soldiers who had distinguished themselves in combat. The third was a bracelet made of copper. Beyond being of Etruscan manufacture, Kendricks thought those last items were worthy as museum pieces with no great intrinsic value. But the necklace.. That, he could not recognise.

Kendricks had no idea what seized him. This was nothing he had ever done before, but without thinking, he took the necklace and placed it in a pocket of his jacket. He had no fears of customs inspections when he returned to England. His reputation as one of the greatest archaeologists in the world guaranteed him a free pass on his return to England. Nobody would dare to challenge him.

As he returned to the front of the tomb, where his colleagues and local staff were gathering, he handed the box to the most senior of the local officers.

The expression of delight on the woman's face was heart-warming.

"What a wonderful addition to our museum," she said and hurried away to begin processing the find.

Kendricks went to his hotel and wrapped the necklace in layers of soft cloth to go at the bottom of his suitcase.

Chapter 3

England

"Welcome home, Dad," said Lisa Kendricks as she got back from school. "How was the trip?"

"Thanks, Sweetie," said Robert Kendricks. He got up from the armchair and embraced his daughter. "It was amazing, like all Etruscan digs are." He released Lisa and resumed his seat, while Lisa sat in the armchair opposite him. "This was back in the huge area called the Tomb of the Sun and the Moon, where you went with me before, and we confirmed what we believed, was that this particular site was the tomb of one of the great Etruscan families. So we found some amazing stuff."

"Oh wow," said Lisa, sensing the excitement in him. "Such as?"

"Some great artworks, even more extraordinary jewelry." Kendricks reached into his briefcase by the side of his chair. "Before your mother gets home, I want to give you something I found. You must promise me you will never tell anyone you have this, and you must never wear it outside the house. I shouldn't have kept it, but somehow, I just knew you had to have it."

He handed it over to Lisa and with excitement, she tore open the package to reveal a beautiful gold necklace.

"Dad!" she exclaimed. "It's amazing. What is it?"

"That was owned by one of the top families in the Etruscan civilization. We found some documents that referred to the family and apparently, they were in a feud with another family that had gone on for several centuries, though we have no idea why. Anyway, Lisa, you must promise what I asked you, never let anyone know you have it, it's probably worth a hundred thousand pounds and I could be fired from my job at the university if it was found out, never mind being charged with a crime and facing prison."

"I promise, Dad," said Lisa. "I'll go and hide it in my room right away."

"Do that," said Kendricks. "Your Mum will be home any minute."

Firmly grasping the necklace, Lisa ran to her room, unlocked the one drawer in her dressing table for which she had a key and placed the beautiful object in it. She locked the drawer and came downstairs just as her mother arrived.

The following day, Lisa came home from school, as usual getting there two hours before either parent returned from work, feeling a growing sense of excitement. Going straight to her room, she unlocked the drawer in her dressing table and took out the golden necklace. Almost immediately, she felt the item grow warm in her hand. Carefully, she fastened it around her neck and stared at her image in the big mirror.

"That's stunning," she murmured. As she looked, she felt the warmth start around her neck and then spread slowly through her whole body. With the warmth was a rush of anger, but she was quite unable to understand just what was causing it. Barely able to breathe, she sat entranced, unaware of the passage of time.

Just for a second, she thought she saw a tiny shadow appear in the mirror, but it vanished. She decided she had imagined it. At some later stage, she heard the front door open as one of her parents arrived. Shaken from the trance, she undid the necklace and returned it to the drawer. Taking a few minutes to regain her composure, she finally went downstairs to find both parents had returned home.

Lisa repeated the process the following afternoon. The same thing happened when she donned the necklace, the growing warmth through her body, the unexplained wave of anger and once again, she thought she saw a brief shadow appear in the mirror.

"All Tarquinia must die," said a soft voice in her ear."

"What? What was that?" gasped Lisa. Nothing answered her. A strange thought entered her mind, the idea of killing somebody. Nothing like that had ever occurred to her before and the idea horrified her. Feeling frightened, she took off the necklace and locked it away. But the memory of the strange voice in her ear and the idea of killing a human being remained in her mind all evening. After dinner, she returned to her room, unwilling to talk with her parents. She tried reading a book but was unable to concentrate.

She slept badly that night.

*   *   *

The following evening, Lisa Kendricks went to her room after dinner, telling her parents that she had homework. Both academic parents accepted that without comment.

Seated before her dressing table mirror, Lisa opened the drawer and extracted the dark blue box. Opening it, she stared at the gold necklace lying there. A small wave of excitement ran through her as she lifted the necklace and carefully fastened it behind her neck. As had happened the two occasions she had worn it, she felt something change in her. The excitement changed to a warm glow, and she stared at her image in the mirror. As she watched, her face seemed to age to adulthood, with powerful determination in her eyes, her jaw line becoming more pronounced and her cheeks growing slimmer.

After the previous occasion she had put on the necklace, the idea of killing a human being had sprung into her mind and now it returned. Slightly shaken by the image, she now was fascinated. This time, it grew from merely an exciting fantasy to a powerful force as she watched. She knew what was going to happen. She replaced the necklace in its box and locked it away.

It was an hour before that force faded and her face in the mirror returned to that of a fourteen-year-old girl

That evening, Lisa again sat before the mirror and donned the necklace. Again, she watched her face change from girlhood to adult and under the excitement, wondered what was happening to her.

"All Tarquinia must die," said the soft voice in her ear again. Somehow, Lisa was not shocked this time. She had no idea what the Tarquinia were, though the name rang a soft bell of memory in her mind, but the conviction grew in her mind that she must somehow kill somebody in the near future. She didn't think about why such a concept would not shock her.

Regretfully, she returned the necklace to its box and in the drawer of the dressing table.

Chapter 4 – Recruiting

England

The two boys were silent as they left the cinema. They were at the bus stop before Dylan broke the deep trance.

"What do you think?" he asked.

Pete took a few moments to get his thoughts in order.

"Stunning," he said eventually. "Somehow, they made killing that guy a real event. I could hardly breathe."

"Exactly what I thought. I realized I was holding my breath the whole time it was happening. When I finally let it out, all I could think of was wondering what it would be like to kill somebody."

"Tell you what," said Pete. "Watching that, I reckon it would be a real buzz."

The bus arrived and the boys said nothing more for the short ride home. Both were deep in thought the entire time and just waved at each other as they made their way to their homes. But when they reached his own rooms, Dylan followed the routine that had been his for months, since he was given the newest computer game.

"Crime Gang Wipeout" was everything he and Pete wanted. Their controller could move personnel from both the cops and the gang members, and they could shoot at opposite personnel, recording kills with direct hits. After over an hour of massive bloodshed, Dylan had recorded twelve kills of the cops and twenty-three of the crime gang. The occasional thought crossed his mind that actually killing criminals would be an awesome experience.

Lisa Kendricks was the cool girl in school. She dressed just a bit better than all the others, with a flair and a style enhanced by expensive clothes made to order for her at a designer in Sydney, paid for by wealthy parents. She didn't officially or obviously date, dating at age fourteen wasn't quite on, but she socialized with the school jocks, the most handsome and the equally wealthy boys. Though occasionally, she managed to sneak into a movie with the coolest boy at school, Jake. So when she walked up to Pete and Dylan sitting on a bench by the playing fields during the lunch break, they were thrown off balance but thrilled at the same time. The two boys were certainly not in the category of "cool" and she had never spoken to them before.

"Hi!" she said cheerfully, directing a wide smile at them and sitting down next to Dylan. But she perched sideways, so she could look at both. "I saw you at the movies yesterday. How did you like it?"

"Er.. great," replied Dylan, his throat dry, shaken by her contact and her nearness to him.

"Great," stammered Pete, unable to take his eyes off her. She was dressed in the standard school uniform, but her skirt was a little shorter than other girls wore theirs and her blue blazer looked well-tailored, hugging her figure in a way that the regular blazers did not. Even at fourteen, she had the curves of a mid-teenager, and her light red hair was bound in a ponytail that was pushed down the side of her neck and over the shoulder, resting on her chest. Both boys found it hard to take their eyes off that ponytail.

"I was there with Jake," she continued, still smiling at them. Jake was the leading jock in Grade nine, sixteen years old and captain of the school rugby team in winter and cricket team in summer. "He didn't like it, the violence and the killing seemed to disturb him. Me, I found it exciting. How about you two?"

The connection with Lisa's reaction and their own eased the shyness in Dylan and Pete.

"Yeah, we thought it was great," said Dylan, finding his voice.

"And we both thought about what it would be like killing somebody," said Pete.

"Oh, wow," exclaimed Lisa and put her hand on Dylan's wrist. "That's what I thought. Can you just imagine it, standing in front of somebody and shooting them, or shoving a knife into their guts and watching their faces as they die? I could hardly sleep last night, thinking about it."

Sharply aware of her hand on his wrist, Dylan couldn't reply, but Pete did.

"Yeah, but we'll never be able to do anything like that. Who could we kill, for a start, and how quickly would we be found out? Cops today have so much technology available, they'd find some clue and we'd spend the rest of our lives in prison."

"I suppose," replied Lisa. "Anyway, there's the bell. What's next, History?" She took her hand off Dylan's wrist, stood up, smoothed down her skirt under the entranced gaze of the two boys and walked quickly away.

Stunned into silence, they followed her into the school building and to their classroom.

Lisa walked into the classroom feeling disturbed. The conversation with Pete and Dylan had been quite unexpected. Why had she approached them? And why did she bring up the topic of killing a person and how enthralling it would be? She had never thought along these lines before. She realised that she had approached the boys because somehow, she had recognised something in them that drove her to the contact. What that was, she could not think. She had no recollection of donning the gold necklace the previous night and the new thoughts that had invaded her mind.

She found it difficult to concentrate on the history lesson. The story of the Spanish Armada and the Royal Navy's destruction of the invading fleet could not compete with the flood of new, strange thoughts taking over her mind.

Chapter 5 – Enhancement

"This is interesting," said Professor Kendricks, studying the collection of papers that had arrived by mail earlier.

"What is?" asked Lisa and her mother simultaneously.

Kendricks put the papers on his lap.

"Remember that second Etruscan tomb my team explored a few weeks ago? I thought we'd found everything there was to be found, but four of that team went back last week for a look at another tomb that they'd explored last year. I knew they were going, they'd asked me, and the Italian government had agreed. Well, it seems they discovered a hidden entrance to another section in that tomb, further underground."

"What have they found?" asked Lisa, feeling oddly moved by the news.

"Nothing yet. They want me to go there and manage the survey, and the University has said the same thing. It has to be a University project, so the head of the department – me - has to lead it."

"So when will you go?" Lisa's mother, also a professor seemed accepting of the situation. The two of them had frequently been away for weeks at a time over the years for such projects.

Kendricks smiled cheerfully.

"The summer break starts next week. Why don't we all go? I'm certain both of you would find it interesting."

Lisa was certain. Somehow, she knew that this expedition was essential to her, though she couldn't identify just why.

"It's an amazing find, Robert," said the archaeology student who had greeted Kendricks and his family at the entrance to the tomb. His youthful face under the shock of red hair reflected the excitement he was expressing. "I really thought we'd completed the search last time. As you know, we were able to translate some words engraved on a slab, this tomb is of the family called Tarquinia, another of the twelve leading families of the Etruscan era."

"It's exciting," agreed Kendricks. "Lead us there, Tom."

The student led the way along one of the two tunnels which had been illuminated by lights strung along the length of them. He came to the end and stopped.

"We thought this was the end," he said. "But one of guys though he saw a tiny line down the right-hand side. It was probably revealed by the vibrations of one of our drills, so we carefully wiped down the wall and found the outline of a doorway, as you see."

He pointed at an almost invisible hairline in the wall and pointed round the outline of a rectangle. He was correct. A barely detectible line now outlined a complete doorway.

"So how do you get in?" asked Kendricks.

"That's the amazing thing. We spent some hours trying to find a handle or some way of pulling it open but look at this." He gently pushed the doorway, and it smoothly slid open inwards without a sound. "That's the most beautifully engineered hinge I have ever seen. Who could have known that somebody could make that over two thousand years ago? This will blow your mind, Robert. You too, Lisa."

"Truly amazing," replied Kendricks and stood aside to allow the team of electrical engineers to take a series of lamp stands into the space revealed.

Her heart pounding, Lisa followed her father into what seemed like a cavernous auditorium, at least three metres high and some twenty metres along each side.

"Lisa, it's safe enough, we can all see each other, so feel free to look around. Shout if you find anything."

The team split up and began walking along the walls, examining every metre. Lisa did the same, studying the wall to her left. There were engravings as far as she could see, pictures of people and animals. Every few metres, there was a small inset cut into the wall. After about an hour of studying, Lisa found one of the insets with a pile of rubble on the ground, where some of the wall had crumbled away. For no reason that she could think of, her heart started thumping again, with a sense of something astounding about to happen. She looked around, all the others were studying the walls intently, taking photographs of the engravings and occasionally calling others to discuss the scenes. She turned to the inset, knelt and began carefully sorting through the small pile of broken wall.

Then it happened. In the pile of dirt and rubble, she saw a small metallic glint. Almost forgetting to breathe, she cleared the debris from around the metal and found it. It was a ring, looking like gold, heavily built, so obviously a man's ring, far too large for a woman. She slipped it onto her index finger of her left hand, the biggest she had, and it was still too large, but something happened.

The warmth in her body that she had experienced when she put on the Etruscan necklace flowed back into her, this time with a greater sense of power. Confused, she took off the ring and slipped it into her pocket, knowing she could not tell her father of the find. She looked a little further along the wall but found nothing else to get her attention. She walked back to join her father and Tom where they were staring with rapt attention at a painting on the wall. She looked at it but saw nothing but what looked like a family group. Oddly, she sensed a spasm of anger run through her but could not think of anything that might cause it.

That evening, the archaeology team was relaxing in the hotel. As the liquor intake grew and the noise level climbed, Professor Kendricks touched Lisa on the shoulder.

"Hey, kid, I suggest it's time for bed for you. Things are getting a bit rowdy here, your mother already called it a day after her shopping marathon."

Lisa laughed. "I think I agree with you. It's past my regular bedtime anyway and it's been an exciting day. Good night."

She stood up, kissed her father on the cheek and left the restaurant. Back in her room, she took out the ring she had discovered. Even holding it caused the same warmth to flood her body as the necklace had caused. She had not brought the necklace with her, fearing possible problems with Customs and Immigration both into Italy and later, back into Britain, but finally, she was unable to resist and slipped the ring back onto her index finger.

The rush of warmth grew sharply, and Lisa felt breathless at the sense of power she had gained. She turned to look at the mirror on the wall and saw her face slowly changing as it had back home when she donned the necklace. She felt that she had grown significantly and the woman in the mirror looked like an adult. Fascinated and excited, she stared at the image for over ten minutes, before realising that she was quite exhausted and needed to sleep. Her father had said he would take her to see a museum of Etruscan relics the next day, and she felt eager to see it. For a few moments she recalled the rush of anger she had experienced when she looked at the painting on the wall. She remembered that she was clutching the large, gold ring she had just found when she saw the painting, but she couldn't imagine any connection between the two. Then she fell asleep.

The museum was unimpressive from the outside, a dull building in dirty red brick and a doorway that was not at all indicative of the history it contained. Inside, it was little better, not the well-displayed treasures that the contents deserved.

After strolling round several areas with Etruscan art, pottery remnants and some jewellery, Kendricks finally led Lisa into another room.

"This is what we got from the tomb we were in during our last expedition. It's the Vulci family tomb with the burial sites of hundreds of the family."

Lisa felt something tugging at her mind. It seemed to be calling her in one direction, and she turned to see what was over there. It looked like another display cabinet.

"What's in there?" she asked.

"That's some of the jewellery we found last time," said Kendricks. "Don't say anything, but that's when we found that necklace I gave you."

"There's nobody else in here, Dad," said Lisa and walked the short distance to the cabinet. Almost immediately she saw a heavy gold ring, identical to the one she had found that morning. She stared at it but felt no connection to it. After looking at several other items, she saw a copper bracelet surrounded by other items, none looking like great treasures. But she couldn't see them, she was transfixed by the copper bracelet. She felt her wrist aching with the need to wear it and she rubbed it slowly.

"What's that?" she asked, pointing at the bracelet.

"Nothing special," said her father. "Only the fact that it's Etruscan gives it value, otherwise, it's just a simple copper bracelet. Actually, I found it together with the ring and that necklace in a box in the tomb of a Vulci family leader in the last expedition."

Lisa continued to stare at it, until her father put his hand on her shoulder.

"Come on, kid, time to rejoin the team at the Tarquinian tomb," he said. "Still lots to see there."

Her wrist still feeling the need to have the bracelet, Lisa and her father returned to rejoin the rest of the archaeology team.

An hour into the continued search of the tomb, Kendricks had another incredible find. Alone in the chamber that housed the preserved body of one of the Tarquinian family, he had a similar experience to that he had in the Vulci tomb. A tiny spot about knee-high on one wall caught his eye. He bent to examine it.

"Could this be the same sort of thing as before in the Vulci tomb?" he said aloud and touched the spot. Not entirely to his surprise, a small panel opened.

"These Etruscans had some astonishing technology," he exclaimed and reached behind the open panel to the small space that it revealed.

Almost he didn't find it, but when his fingers encountered the smooth touch of linen, he took hold and pulled out a small roll of the material.

"What in Earth..? he muttered. He could barely make out under the surface that there was some form of marking. Not wishing to possibly harm the marks by unrolling ancient material, he carefully stashed the little roll into his bag.

Later in his room, he sat at his table. Unrolling ancient documents was a skill he had perfected through years of practice and now he focused his attention on the linen roll. Using tweezers and intense care, he finally unrolled the delicate material to reveal several lines of writing. Immediately, he recognised it.

"It's Greek," he said aloud. "This is extraordinary. We knew that Greek was known to many Etruscans, but this is something remarkable."

Like all senior archaeologists, Kendricks could read ancient Greek, if slowly and carefully, and occasionally he referred to his laptop for assistance with an unknown word, but finally he reached something that amazed him.

"This is a ritual to raise a demon," he said, feeling a shock of astonishment. "What the hell..?"

A few lines further, reading into the detailed steps described, a bigger shock hit him as the text prescribed walking round a sacrificed body in an anticlockwise direction.

"They walk Widdershins! Good grief, this is the same routine used in Medieval Britain when worshipping Satan. How could these two different civilisations have the same rituals?"

There was yet another shock. A few lines further down, there was a section written in another language, one that Kendricks could not at all identify. It bore no resemblance to anything he had ever seen before and he was well-experienced in several ancient written languages from Sumerian, though Arabic, Egyptian hieroglyphics and Aramaic.

"Where the hell did this thing come from?" he exclaimed.

With a surge of excitement, Kendricks realised that he almost certainly had a massive research project ahead of him that could take years. Finally, well after two in the morning, he wrapped up the document and stored it securely in his suitcase.

Two days later, Lisa and her mother returned home, leaving the students to complete the examination and documentation of the newly discovered hall under the direction of Professor Kendricks.

Lisa did not enjoy travelling with her mother or even being together with her for any length of time. She had never felt any closeness with her, unlike her father to whom she was very close. The entire flight on the

British Airways plane was mostly in silence with few comments outside thoughts on what meal to order or what was expected when school started again the next term. Lisa had hidden the ring as well as she could, but as usual, the family of the renowned professor Robert Kendricks was known to the Immigration and Customs staff and she and her mother were waved through without a pause.

On reaching home, Lisa retired to her room to spend time admiring the ring. She didn't don the gold necklace but sensed the similarities in reaction between wearing either item. For a moment, she recalled the sense of longing when she saw the copper bracelet and wondered just why that was.

But in a sudden flash of memory, she recalled why the name of the Tarquinia Family rang a bell in her mind. Her father had briefly mentioned it during their first visit to the tomb, but another memory shook her.

"All Tarquinia must die," the whispered voice had said in her room.

Lisa realised that she was involved in something different from any normal experience.

* * *

Three days later, with her father still in Italy and her mother at a staff meeting of the university, Lisa moved to her room, feeling a mix of excitement and fear. Sitting at her dressing table, she extracted the golden necklace and put it round her neck.

Once more, she felt the wave of warmth and power sweep through her body as she watched her face change from little girl to adult and felt her body following, growing into a woman's body. Unable to stop now, she pulled the ring from the same drawer, and slid it onto the index finger,

If the changes that had followed her donning the necklace were powerful, the new surge in her was a frightening increase. Lisa sat and stared at her image as the face became even more of an adult, now reflecting charismatic power, the eyes becoming quite magnetic. She trembled with a mix of awe and fear, totally mesmerised by what was happening to her.

A small spot appeared in the image. Almost unable to move, Lisa watched as the spot grew and became the shadowy image of a young woman. Her clothes looked strange in the brief moment Lisa had, but she couldn't identify them. The shock broke her immobility, and she turned to look behind her.

There was nobody there.

Gasping for breath through lungs that seemed to be blocking the air, Lisa turned back to the mirror. The image of the woman was still there. She moved slightly, raising one hand in greeting.

"Hello, Lisa," she said. "Thank you for summoning me. It's been a long time."

"Who are you?" Lisa managed to rasp through a dry mouth.

"I am Anna Vulci," said the image.

"Vulci?" she gasped. "But we were…"

"Just in my enemy's tomb. And you have a necklace and a ring that were taken from us."

"But why…?" Lisa was unable to say more.

"Why am I here and how did you summon me?"

She nodded.

"My family had been in a blood feud with the Tarquinia family for centuries before the Etruscans became merged with the Romans. Before my father died, he summoned a demon and it cursed the ring and the necklace, saying the owner would kill the Tarquinia for as long as any of them lived. Many still do."

"But how…?

"Putting on the two pieces has made you the owner and now you have all the powers of the demon that cursed them and only you can summon me. And you are now charged with killing any of the Tarquinia family that you can find. But you will need one more thing to become truly a Vulci assassin."

"What is that?"

"You will know when you are ready."

It was all too much for Lisa. She removed the ring and the necklace, put both back in the drawer. She looked back at the mirror. The woman had gone. So too had the feelings of power and her appearance was slowly returning to that of a fourteen-year-old girl.

Lisa burst into tears for reasons she could not identify.

Chapter 6 – Enlightenment

Two days passed before Lisa met the two boys again. In that time, both boys were obsessed with the memory of how Lisa had approached them, sat with them and talked about doing something truly exciting.

Pete was haunted by the memory of how she stood up, smoothed down her short skirt over her legs and walked away, Dylan by the memory of her hand on his wrist and her closeness as she sat next to him. They sat on the same bench by the playing field as before, watching the school rugby team practicing. Pete was watching Jake, the captain, despite being two years younger than the most senior boys. It was painful for him, knowing that he dated Lisa, even though she was only fourteen. Jealousy ran through him like cold water.

Both boys had their difficulties at school, mainly with sports. Dylan was heavily built, had no athletic abilities at all. Pete was slight, too small to handle any contact sports and neither had the reflexes or reaction times to play other sports like tennis. Neither had ever been picked for a class team or a warm-up team for any sports at all.

"It was weird how she just came and talked to us about killing somebody," said Dylan.

"Well, I wish she'd do it again," replied Pete.

"God, she's coming," grated Dylan, tension hitting him like a punch.

Pete couldn't say anything, his throat dry as the dust at their feet. They watched as she approached, unable to avoid looking at her legs as they were displayed under the short skirt flapping in the breeze.

She arrived and sat down on the bench between the two boys.

"Jake's pretty good, isn't he?" she said brightly. "A real athlete."

"Er.. yes," replied Dylan, his throat tight.

She seemed to ignore the tension radiating from the two boys.

"I've been doing some reading about what we were talking about," she continued. "It looks like when a body is discovered, the cops send in a special team led by somebody called the Scene of Crime Officer. They refer to him or her as "SOCO." They wear special clothing to make sure they don't mess up the area and lose any clues they might find."

Pete found his voice. "Yes, I've seen that a few times. My dad likes to watch the British cop shows like *'Inspector Morse'* and *'Inspector Frost'* and they always send in a SOCO."

"Me too," chimed in Dylan. "They wear a complete overall thing, covers everything from head to toe, gloves, face mask and something over their feet so as not to leave footprints."

"That's it," exclaimed Lisa, showing excitement and looking side to side at both boys. "So now you know what we'll need."

"What? What do you mean, what we'll need?" Dylan was stunned by her comment.

"Come on, guys, we've gone so far, we've agreed we'd love to kill somebody and now I've done the research on how to do it without leaving clues for the cops." Lisa had become very animated, sitting upright instead of leaning against the back of the bench and her gaze at each of the boys had become intense. "You know we want to do it, and I know how to do it, as well."

Despite their confusion and some fear, neither Pete nor Dylan could deny their intrigue. Much of it was from having the coolest girl at school talking to them in such a manner, but there was a definite attraction in what she was saying.

Their silence encouraged Lisa to continue.

"It needs to be somebody that nobody really cares about," she said. "So it can't be somebody like a parent of somebody here at the school, or a business type, they'd get intensive police attention if one of them got killed. No, the best one would be one of the homeless people who sleep in the streets or just out of town. They have no relatives, no friends, nobody would miss one of them."

Both boys stared at her, open-mouthed. But underneath the shock of what she was saying, both of them were fascinated and excited.

"How would we do it?" Dylan managed to say.

"First, we have to get the coverall things," Lisa said. "There are two hardware stores that sell them here, I went into them at the weekend and checked. The best bet is you go in at different times, one of you buys two."

"Why us, why not you?" asked Pete.

"It's the sort of things blokes buy. I'd be noticed and somebody would be more likely to recall seeing a girl getting one."

Pete nodded. "I suppose so."

"And you can buy a pair of industrial gloves," Lisa continued.

"Where are we supposed to get the money for these things?" Dylan seemed doubtful about the idea. "I don't have enough to buy them."

Lisa shook her head impatiently. "I'll give you the money. I've got quite a lot. My dad gives me good pocket money, and I've earned a bit doing some sewing for my aunt and a couple of my Mum's friends. I'm quite good at making dresses and things."

"And what about covering our feet?" Pete was becoming increasingly intrigued by what was developing.

"I'll make them," said Lisa. "It just needs to be a cloth bag big enough to go over your shoes and up to your ankles and tied round your leg with string. I've got a sewing machine in my room, I'll make them all in about an hour. And just to make sure, before you put the bags on, put football socks on over the shoes, make sure there's no way of leaving identifying footprints."

Lisa had them totally under control now and both boys were beginning to sense rising excitement at the prospect of what they were talking about actually happening.

"Your dad must be pretty rich," said Dylan. "What does he do?

"He's a history professor at the university. He specialises in ancient European history and one of his things is Etruscan history. He's written several books about that."

"What's Etruscan?" asked Pete.

"A strange civilisation that lived in northern Italy some centuries before Christ. They were dominant, but nobody really knows where they came from, nobody has properly understood their language and they only faded away as the Romans began to build an Empire and take over the world. My dad is probably the greatest expert on them. He went on several expeditions to explore Etruscan tombs and found massive amounts of artifacts and jewellery and stuff like that. They're in museums all over the world."

"Wow," said Dylan.

"Yeah, he gave me one beautiful necklace, it's worth thousands, so I only wear it at home and in my room, because my dad said I must never wear it when I go out, it's too valuable. He got it in a tomb called the Tomb of the Sun and the Moon, built for one of the massively rich Etruscan families called the Vulci. Dad shouldn't have taken it, but nobody saw him take it and it was never catalogued, so nobody even knows it's missing."

"Wow," said Dylan again.

Lisa had got into her stride and was speaking with passion and excitement. The boys were happy to listen to and look at her.

"He did another tomb also, one for a family called the Tarquinia. And what got him excited was to decipher parts of some of the documents there which told about the feud with the Vulci that had gone on for decades. So he went back to the Vulci tomb and was able to translate a few scraps of parchment which also talked about that feud. And what's more, it talked about the necklace Dad gave me. He said it's apparently cursed by a demon who will kill the Tarquinia family."

"Aren't you afraid to wear it?" Pete looked worried.

"Nah, I don't believe all that stuff." Lisa had calmed down. "Back to the real topic. I'll bring money into school tomorrow, so you can buy the overalls, okay?"

The two boys nodded. They had obviously accepted Lisa as the leader of their group.

"Okay, back to class," she said. "Maths, isn't it?"

That evening, Lisa retreated to her room as soon as she could, claiming a homework load. She sat at her dresser, pulled open the drawer and donned the necklace. Immediately, she felt a rush of warmth and power as she watched her image slowly change to one of a young woman. Then she slipped the large, gold ring over her index finger and felt the power increase even more. This time, with the increased power, came a rush of anger, a deep need to kill a human being. Frightened by this, she was about to take off the ring when the image of the woman appeared.

"Leave it," she commanded.

"What's happening?' Lisa asked, her voice trembling.

"You are about to fulfil your destiny," said the woman.

"My.. destiny?"

"Lisa, you are a killer, a natural killer. We have seen that in you since you were born and now you can begin to do what you were born to do."

"Is that why I talked to Pete and Dylan like that today? I didn't really know what I was saying."

"You were speaking from your innermost soul. You found two boys who shared your compulsion to kill and now all of you can satisfy the deep need. Another time, I will tell you an even greater truth about you."

"What must I do?"

"Finish what you have started with your friends."

Sensing both excitement and fear in herself, Lisa took off the ring and the necklace. Somehow, she knew that the next day would start her fulfillment.

Chapter 7 – First Blood

"What have you told your parents?" Lisa handed over the two bags for their feet and the three of them sat in an alleyway well away from populated areas. Dark had fallen over an hour ago and there was no moon visible behind the heavy clouds.

"We both said we were going to running training at the sports ground." Jason began wrapping string round his ankles, securing the cloth bag in place.

"And that's really happening," added Pete. "The place is floodlit and lots of people do it. There's a football match in the middle, so there'll be lots of people in the stands. So if they ask any other parents about it, they'll know there was a practice session, even if nobody can actually remember that we were there. What about you?"

"I said I was going to the movies." Lisa had finished tying up her shoe covers and was walking around to test the security. "My friend Joanne is going, so she'll tell me all about it, in case Mum and Dad ask me. We do this quite often, so they're used to it, and they won't be suspicious. Okay, are you guys done?"

The two boys stood up and followed Lisa's example of walking around to test their bindings, closely watched by her.

"Looks good," she said.

"Lisa, are we really going to do this?" Pete sounded frightened, his voice hoarse.

"You're darned sure we are." Lisa flourished a large carving knife she had taken from a scabbard round her waist. "And this is what we'll use. I sharpened it up yesterday before Mum and Dad got home from work. When we get back tonight, I'll hide it in the garden, then tomorrow, I'll run it through the dishwasher and put it back in the kitchen. Nobody will ever suspect a thing."

Pete still looked worried.

"Pete, don't go wobbly on me," said Lisa. "You know you want to do this." She walked over to him, put her arms round his neck and hugged him. "There, does that feel better?"

Pete said nothing but the look on his face indicated that she had completely enslaved him.

"You okay, Dylan?" she asked.

Dylan seemed more confident and nodded. "Okay, what's next?" he asked.

"Okay, are you sure you have nothing that could drop off to provide a clue to SOCO?" she demanded. "No wallet, no watch, nothing?"

The boys shook their heads.

"I left everything behind also," she said. "No jewellery, no watch."

She was not being truthful. Before leaving the house, she had put the gold necklace round her neck and the ring in her pocket, not trusting it on her hand where it could fall, and stood silently for ten minutes, feeling the surge of strange power fill her body. Nothing could stop her now.

All three were silent for a moment, preparing for the critical moment.

"Follow me," she said. If there had ever been any doubt about who was in charge, there was none now. Lisa was as much in command as an army officer leading troops into combat. "I've been around here a few times," she continued. "There's lots of homeless old tramps sleeping rough, and they all seem to have their regular positions. There's one, sleeps in a doorway well out of sight of the others and we can get to him without going by any of the others, so nobody will see us."

Confidently, she led the others down several alleyways in what had once been a residential area but was now deserted as the buildings aged and became decrepit. Abruptly, she stopped, turned to the two boys and held her finger before her mouth. She signalled and raised the hood of her coverall after placing a black cloth mask over the lower half of her face. Obediently, the boys did the same.

Lisa pointed at a darkened doorway a few metres away. Barely discernible was a huddled pile of what looked like old clothing. The three walked up to it and Lisa kicked it. The pile moved and a face appeared from under a blanket. The face was dirty, bearded and the eyes barely opened.

"Wha…" grunted the face's owner.

"Wake up, you filthy old bastard," said Lisa and kicked him again.

This time, the man sat up, slowly and painfully. "What do you want?" he mumbled.

Lisa reached inside her overall and pulled out the knife. With a quick movement, she pushed the knife into the festering shirt that covered the man's chest. He gasped, moaned and clutched his chest. Lisa pulled out the knife, gestured to Dylan to take it. With just a small hesitation, Dylan repeated the strike, pulled out the knife and tried to hand it to Pete, but Pete backed away, waving his hands in refusal.

"Dammit," said Lisa, took the knife, bent down and drew it across the man's throat. Blood poured from the wound. Lisa stood up and watched, a smile across her face. Dylan also stood motionless, watching the dying man's final moment while Pete seemed frozen, his hands up to his mouth.

Finally, the old man fell sideways, clearly dead.

"Go," snapped Lisa and led the way out of the alley. A few hundred metres away, they stopped. All three removed their foot coverings, overalls, and masks. Lisa pulled a large garbage bag from a pocket of her overall.

"Everything in here," she ordered. Obediently, the boys followed her example and put their overalls, masks and foot coverings into the bag.

"I don't think any blood got onto anything," she said, "but tomorrow I'll put them through the washing machine at home twice, maybe three times and that will remove any trace of anything. Let's go."

Cautiously, they worked their way back to populated areas, saw nobody and then the reactions hit.

"Omigod, omigod, omigod," exclaimed Dylan and raised his hands to a high-five with Pete who seemed to have recovered from his shock.

"Hoo-whee," shouted Pete. "That was bloody incredible. We actually did it."

"We sure did," joined in Lisa. She seemed to be glowing with happiness. "That was everything I thought it would be."

"We have to do it again," said Dylan, exhilaration making him dance on the sidewalk.

"We will," replied Lisa. "But not for a while. Let's see what happens next, if the cops put any real effort into the case and if they think of possible suspects."

"They won't, will they?" Dylan stopped dancing and looked anxiously at her.

"No chance," she said. "Anyway, let's get away from here, just in case somebody drives past and remembers seeing three kids celebrating something. And I have to get home and make sure all this stuff gets hidden until I can get it all clean. See you at school."

All of them made their ways home. Dylan and Pete found it hard to sleep that night. Lisa had no such difficulty.

Chapter 8 – Second Blood

Two weeks later, Pete and Dylan were again sitting on a bench by the playing field, though no players were practicing, as Lisa observed them from near the school building. She felt her own emotions and could only sense excitement and some confusion. While she could remember the experience of watching herself in the mirror change and grow older, and the rush of warmth through her body as she donned the necklace and ring, she had no memory of seeing the image of a woman appear and talk to her. After a few moments, she began walking to where the boys were sitting.

Neither boy said anything as she approached, though their reactions were strong. Pete stood up, Dylan remained seated, but both boys' bodies were rigid with tension.

Lisa sat down next to Dylan and gestured to Pete to sit on her other side.

"Time we did it again," she said.

Dylan drew in his breath with a small sound, Pete did not react.

"When?" asked Dylan.

"Tomorrow night," Lisa replied. "Let's do it the same way, that's the easiest."

"Do we meet in the same place?" asked Pete, breaking his silence.

"We do. I'll bring the foot covers, you bring your overalls. It's Saturday, so you should be able to tell your parents you'll be at the movies together. Tell them you're seeing "Gladiator II." I saw it last night with Jake, so I'll tell you all about it, then if your parents ask you about it, you can tell them, and they'll believe you were there."

Dylan and Pete were now completely under Lisa's control and leadership. Both sensed that she had changed since the last murderous episode, she had somehow grown in personality. But they also knew that they had themselves changed. There were no doubts in their minds, they looked forward with excitement to the following night.

"Ready?" said Lisa.

The three children were in the same spot where they had met the previous time. All the buildings around were empty, unlit, several in serious states of collapse. The deep gloom surrounded them.

"Foot covers on? Masks on? Gloves on?" Lisa ran through the checks in the same, cool manner as a pilot completing the pre-take-off check. Satisfied that they were all ready, she led them back along the same route they had taken before. Several sleeping bodies were huddled in places along the way, but Lisa confidently led them to a building apart from the others. She forced open the door and used her flashlight to search the room in which they found themselves. In one corner, a shapeless mass was lying under a pile of old newspapers.

Lisa walked up to the shape and kicked away most of the newspapers to reveal an old man in dirty old clothes. She shone the light into his face, and he woke up, mumbling, trying to hide his eyes from the light.

"What...?" he finally said.

Lisa knelt down and plunged her knife into the man's neck. Blood spurted out and covered his front.

"Pete, your turn," Lisa said and held the knife out to him.

Without hesitation, Pete took the knife and with a hard stroke, slammed it into the blood-covered chest. The man screamed, and the scream faded into a rasping bubbly gasp. Pete laughed and repeated the blow.

"Let Dylan have a go," ordered Lisa. Dylan didn't hesitate, took the knife and sliced it across the old man's neck. This time, the old man made no noise. He raised his hands as if pleading to be left, but in seconds, he collapsed, obviously dead.

"Yay!" exclaimed Dylan. "That was great."

"Let's get going," commanded Lisa and they walked out of the old house, back onto the narrow street. But things did not go smoothly.

"What are you people doing?" The voice was a weak rasp and came from another old tramp walking along the street. "Who are you?"

He got no further. Still holding the knife, Dylan jumped on the man and thrust the blade into the man's stomach. The derelict old man let out a gasp of pain and clutched his body. Dylan laughed and repeated the blow, then stood aside as the man slowly sank to the ground.

"Well done," said Lisa. "Now, let's get going."

Chapter 9 – The Homicide Squad

"What have we got?" Detective Inspector Adrian Cooper was irritated.

"Almost nothing," replied Detective Constable Mary Stanton. "Three knifing murders of homeless old derelicts, and not a single clue that we can use. The only thing we know is that it's the same knife each time, the blade is eighteen centimetres long and three centimetres wide, only one cutting edge."

"So your common or garden domestic carving knife," said Cooper.

"Exactly," said Stanton.

Cooper looked at Detective Sergeant James Brigham, seated next to Stanton.

"Anything to add to that, Sergeant.

Brigham shook his head. "She's got it," he said.

Cooper knew better than to demand more details. He and Stanton had become accustomed to the sparse contribution from their colleague. Unlike many, he seemed not to need the limelight and was happy to leave others to take centre stage.

"And nothing else," continued Stanton. "We've not found a single clue to the identity of the killer or killers. No footprints, no fingerprints, no bloodstains, other than the victim's, no DNA." All one point eight metres of her slender frame radiated frustration.

"They must be wearing standard SOCO protection gear," said Cooper. "Whoever this is, he, she or they have thoroughly prepared."

"Easy enough," said Stanton. "Every cop show on tv these days makes it clear that full cover is required. Hell, watch three episodes of *"Silent Witness,"* you have a complete tutorial in how to kill somebody without leaving a clue."

"But that certainly means these killings are planned and prepared," said Cooper. "What do we know about the victims?"

"Only that they were all derelicts, homeless blokes living rough in the abandoned part of the town. We took DNA samples to try and identify them without luck so far." Sadness was strong in Mary Stanton's face. "We're going through years of missing persons reports, but it's almost hopeless."

"Want to add to that, Sergeant?" asked Cooper.

Brigham shook his head. Cooper gave up and looked at Mary.

"Any more from the pathologist?" he asked.

"Actually, there is a bit," said Stanton. "Your comment about he, she or they being the culprits. Definitely multiple killers. Doctor Cowdroy said the knife blows were different depths and at different angles. He thinks at least two killers, one with more certainty and confidence than the other."

"He thinks it could be one more forceful killer, another who might be on his or her first experience?" Cooper became a little more involved.

"That's what he said," agreed Mary.

"Shit, what a mess," said Cooper. "Okay, we've increased patrols in the abandoned area where the three were killed, but I doubt there'll be any more there, if we think they've graduated to more challenging game. Step up the house-to-house calls, talk to more of the homeless, see if anyone saw anything at all in the area or nearby."

The two detectives nodded and left the Inspector's office.

Chapter 10 – Continued Growth

"That was bloody amazing," said Dylan. The two boys were sitting with Lisa on a bench by the football field as the school team practiced. "I've never felt such a thrill as when that old bloke collapsed when I stabbed him, all on my own."

"Same with me," said Pete, rubbing his hands together. "When Lisa hit the first one first with the jab in his neck, the way the blood flowed was amazing. I never knew we had so much blood in our bodies. Just as well we had the overalls and foot covers, we'd have a problem washing it off, otherwise."

"You guys did well," said Lisa. "You're getting more competent with each one. Maybe I'll let one of you make the first hit next time."

"Next time?" Pete looked interested. "Have you got any ideas about what we'll do for the next one?"

"One thought," said Lisa. "I think it would be even more exciting if the victim knew what was coming before we kill them."

"Oh wow!" Dylan raised his fist into the air. "What a turn on. Yes, just imagine it. Somehow, we have the guy tied up somewhere and we show him the knife for a while before we kill him. Can you imagine the face he'd pull?"

"No need for it to be a man," said Lisa. "We haven't killed a woman yet. Maybe it's time we did."

Dylan looked doubtful. "Not sure about killing a woman," he said. "It would have to be an old one, I really can't fancy killing a young woman or a girl."

"Don't get wussy," scoffed Lisa. "If we're going to be serious about this, we have to cover the spectrum, young people, old people, men, women."

They were interrupted by the arrival of Jake off the playing field. He was covered in mud and there was a streak of blood down his left leg. He looked irritated.

"What are you three talking about?" he demanded. "Lisa, I thought we were going for an ice-cream after the practice. What are you doing with these two losers?"

"Stop worrying, Jake. I can talk with anyone I want, you don't own me," Lisa snapped sharply, her own irritation showing.

"Well, are we, or aren't we?" retorted Jake. He glared down at Dylan and Pete. "Why don't you two idiots clear off, so I can talk to my girl?"

Feeling intimidated by the large, muscular Jake, the two boys looked at Lisa for guidance. She nodded, and Dylan and Pete moved away.

"I hate that bastard," said Dylan.

"Maybe we can kill him next?" replied Pete.

"I'd like that, but Lisa probably won't let us."

They were silent as they returned to the school, lost in their own thoughts.

* * *

"I did a lot of research for this one." Lisa put a chocolate in her mouth as she and the two boys sat behind a large bush on the outside of a poorly maintained garden a short distance out of town. "She lives alone, just a cat with her and as you can see, there's not another house within a hundred metres. She plays her tv very loud, so nobody is going to hear us when we go in."

"How are we going to do that?" asked Pete.

"We break the kitchen window. We'll wait until we hear her tv go on, and then we can crack the window gently and climb in. She won't hear a thing."

"Great," exclaimed Dylan.

"And there will be a bonus," continued Lisa. "It's pension day, she collected hers this morning, so unless she's spent some already, there'll be a few hundred pounds at least."

They subsided into silence for ten minutes, and then the sound of the television reached them clearly.

"Nice and dark," said Lisa. "Got your gear on correctly?"

"Yes," replied the boys in unison and all three stood up. They entered the garden through the small gate that was half open and walked up to the kitchen. One small window was the sole entry. Lisa took a towel from her pocket, and using a stone she had picked up during their wait, gently tapped the stone on the towel against the glass. After a few sharp taps, a small section of glass fell away. Using the gap, Lisa held the pane and struck it again. As it cracked, she carefully pulled the pane away and placed it on the floor. She repeated the process until the whole window had been removed.

"That was clever," said Dylan. "I wouldn't have thought of that."

Lisa didn't reply but gestured to him to help her up and climb through the window. Once in, she opened the back door, and the two boys walked in. The sound of the television shrouded any noise, and they followed it to the room at the front. Opening the door, they could see an old woman sitting in an armchair, a glass of something in her hand, facing the large tv screen. She saw them at the same moment and screamed, the glass dropping from her hand and spilling the contents on her dress.

Lisa pointed at a dining table chair and Dylan pulled it away from the table. Pete and Lisa grabbed the old woman and without any difficulty lifted the tiny frame from her armchair and placed her in the upright chair. Lifting a line of thin rope from round her neck, she and the two boys used it to tie the woman firmly to the chair and her hands behind her.

She was trying to say something, but her weak voice was lost in the television's racket, though her face reflected extreme terror.

Lisa took the knife from the sheath at her chest, and pointed to Pete, indicating he should take it. As he advanced on the old woman, she screamed, loud enough to be heard over the noise of the tv. The three killers stood and watched, entranced by the fear radiating from her, then Pete plunged the weapon into her chest over the heart. She stared at him as the light rapidly went from her eyes.

Dylan seized the knife, pulled it from the woman's chest and slammed it into the other side. He looked at Lisa, but she shook her head.

For a few moments, they studied the scene, obviously entranced. Then Lisa looked around, saw the woman's handbag and opened it, pulling out a wad of banknotes. Not bothering to count it, she waved at the boys and the three of them walked out to the kitchen, out of the back door and through the garden gate again.

* * *

Back in her bedroom, Lisa sat on the side of the bed, experiencing a deep sense of satisfaction. The killing of the old lady had left her fulfilled and she felt delighted that her tutelage of Dylan and Pete had resulted in their initiation into the art of murder.

"Now it is time for you to move on to your dedicated career," said a woman's voice.

Startled, Lisa turned to see the woman who had called herself Anna Vulci sitting on a chair in the corner of the room. She looked perfectly normal, Lisa struggled to realise that she was the spirt of a woman from over two thousand years ago. Somehow, she radiated power and menace and she disturbed Lisa badly.

"What does that mean?" Lisa asked. "Dedicated career?"

"Your entire life is dedicated to killing members of the Tarquinia Family. We placed that curse on them, and the curse is carried by three items of jewellery. You have two of them. I told you before that you need one more thing to be complete as the killer of Tarquinia. Now is the time for you to have it."

Despite the fear that the woman caused in her, Lisa could not withstand the surge of interest.

"What is it?" she asked.

"Hold out your left hand," said the woman.

Lisa did so and immediately saw the copper bracelet she had last seen in the museum in Italy. It encircled her wrist, and she felt the warm glow that previously she had experienced when she donned the necklace and the ring.

"But.. how?" she gasped. "I saw it in the museum. How did you..?"

The woman ignored the question. "Put on the other two items," she ordered.

Lisa opened the drawer of the dressing table and pulled out the two items. First, she slid the ring onto one finger and clenched her fist to hold it in place. The body warmth grew stronger, and she felt the first rush of killing lust. When she donned the necklace, her whole body erupted with furious energy. Now she knew what she was born to do. She would kill Tarquinia. She stared at the woman named Anna Vulci who smiled at her.

"And now you know," she said. "With all three items, you will always be able to tell a Tarquinian, even after more than two thousand years, the smell of that evil tribe will be sensed by you, and you will know that you must kill the one you have seen."

The woman vanished. Lisa continued to sit, experiencing the exhilarating sensation of being the killer of all members of an ancient Etruscan tribe.

Chapter 11 – The Vulci Curse

"We have a guest at our assembly today, boys and girls," said the Principal. "Mr Graham Adams is a retired Major General in our army and has seen military combat in several theatres of war during his career. What is especially noteworthy is that today is General Adams' one hundredth birthday. So please welcome this extraordinary man to talk to us today."

The Principal turned and gestured at the man sitting in a chair at the back of the stage with the other teachers. The man stood up and walked to the front of the stage, showing no signs of difficulty moving.

Lisa felt admiration for the speaker who didn't look remotely as old as his one hundredth birthday would indicate. He stood straight, looked very fit, with no surplus weight that she could see.

"Good morning, boys and girls," said the old soldier.

As soon as he spoke, Lisa's admiration faded to be replaced by a surge of fury. She was bewildered. Why was she so angry? She tried to concentrate on the words coming from him, but she could make no sense of them, losing any meaning in the fury that filled her body. When the old man finished speaking, the children broke into loud applause. Looking around, Lisa saw many excited faces, boys and girls, who seemed enthralled by what the General had said.

"Thank you, General Adams," said the Principal as the old soldier returned to his seat. "The General will visit some of our classes during the day," she continued. "So if you have any questions for him, that will be the time to ask them."

The assembly ended and the students filed out to return to their classrooms and the lessons of the day

Lisa tried to concentrate on the two classes, History and English before the morning break, but all she could think of was why had she been so angry when Adams began speaking. She had never experienced such a flood of fury and hatred, and it made no sense to her. But she recalled the small wave of anger she had felt in the Tarquinia tomb. It had felt similar, but today's fury far exceeded the previous one. She sat alone during the break, ignoring Jake when he came to sit next to her, but spoke briefly to Dylan and Pete when they approached her.

"What did you think of the old bloke?" asked Dylan. "I thought he was fantastic, I've never heard anyone describe warfare so well. What did you think, Lisa?"

Lisa just shook her head, irritated by the intrusion. The two boys were about to say more, but the bell rang for the next class.

As everyone walked out of the school at 4:00pm, Lisa saw a young woman walking out with the General, leading him to a car parked by the main entrance and driving off. Inexplicably, Lisa felt something of the same anger when she saw the woman, but it was overwhelmed by the rush of hatred when she looked at the General. She remained confused by what had happened.

At home, she went to her room and switched on her laptop computer and began looking for information about Major General Graham Adams. There was plenty to see, a full record of his service and his earlier life at school and at the Royal Military College at Sandhurst. But that was of no interest to Lisa. What grabbed attention was the single statement that the General lived in the same area as Lisa. She switched to the White Pages directory on her computer and found him within minutes, his address and telephone number clearly displayed.

Lisa switched off the computer as she heard her parents come home and prepared to join them for dinner.

Two hours later, back in her room before the dressing table mirror, she took out the Etruscan jewellery and put on all three pieces, immediately sensing the power flooding into her as her image in the mirror grew from a young girl to an adult woman. Also in the mirror was the young Vulci woman.

"Now you have entered my world," said the shadow image.

"What? How have I done that?"

"You learnt that last evening. But you know what you have to do. It's time to grow up from killing old tramps and women and move to a higher level."

"I don't understand," said Lisa. "What higher level? I don't know what you are telling me." But as she said that, she remembered how she had acquired the copper bracelet the previous evening and become fully aware of what she must do.

"Yes, you do," replied the shadow and disappeared.

Lisa realised that she really did know and the information both enthralled and frightened her, and she understood why the arrival of the General had so enraged her.

*   *   *

"Friday night," said Lisa.

"Fantastic," exclaimed Dylan and Pete nodded enthusiastically. "The same place?"

"Not this time. We're moving up to a higher level now."

"What does that mean?" asked Pete.

"You'll find out, but you're going to love it. Here's what you do. Bring all the gear with you, get the six pm 435 bus, but we must get on it at different places. I'll get on at the depot, you two check on bus stops. Lots of people get on that bus then, going home from work, it goes to a residential area, so there'll be kids from the high school also. Nobody will notice us if we're not obviously together. Get off at Blaxland Street and go straight into the woods nearby. We'll wait there till it gets dark."

"Sounds exciting," said Pete. "Who are we going to kill?"

"You'll find out then," said Lisa, stood up and began to walk away.

"She's incredible," said Dylan and Pete could only nod his agreement.

* * *

"It's that old geezer that spoke to us," said Lisa as the three sat behind a thick bush in the woods, waiting for night to fall.

"The General?" Dylan was severely shocked. "Why him?"

"We need to move up," said Lisa. "Killing old tramps that nobody cares about was too easy, there's no thrill in that after the first two or three. And the old woman, she was just a better practice."

"Yes, but the General.." Dylan's dismay was obvious.

"Getting wobbly, Dylan? Losing your nerve? How about you, Pete?"

Neither boy answered at first but looked at each other for a few moments before a decision was made.

"We're with you," said Dylan.

"Good,' said Lisa. "Now, get the overalls and shoe covers on, we'll go in five minutes."

The entry to the General's house posed no difficulties. The kitchen door was unlocked and there were no signs of anyone but the old man living there. They heard the television and followed the noise to the lounge room. The General was sitting in an armchair watching the television, but he showed his awareness of intruders.

"What are you children doing here?" he asked, looking undisturbed. He peered closely at Lisa, and she felt the same surge of anger and hatred as their eyes met.

"We've come to kill you," she replied, struggling to keep her voice under control.

Dylan moved away and circled the armchair, staying a metre or more away. Lisa saw him take out a box cutter from one pocket and extend the blade.

"And just why would a bunch of children want to do that?" The General seemed quite calm. "But I know you, you were at the school this morning."

Lisa could not understand the fury raging through her, but she was past caring. Only the need to kill was dominant. She watched as Dylan moved closer to the armchair until he was close behind Adams, the blade in his hand. She extracted her knife and advanced on the old man who watched her closely. As she drove the knife at the General's throat, he moved faster than she could ever have managed. His hand leaped out from his hip, as fast as a snake striking, holding a heavy blade. He slashed at Lisa's hand, cutting a deep slice in her forearm. She screamed, just as Dylan cut the man's throat from behind.

Lisa retreated, clutching her arm as blood dripped from it, leaving some on the carpet. The General stared at her, apparently without emotion, then the light faded from his brilliant blue eyes, and he sagged back into the armchair.

Lisa raced into the kitchen and found a tea towel, wrapped it round her arm and somehow stemmed the blood flow.

"Let's get out of here," she said, and they rapidly left the house and back into the woods.

"I need to get this looked at," she said, trying to keep calm. "All of us, get out of our overalls and foot covers, put them all in the one bag. Dylan, you keep that until I can get them washed again. Now let's get going."

They moved back to the main road and found a bus stop quite close. Fortunately, a bus arrived within minutes and Lisa was able to reach the emergency ward of the local hospital. Her conversation with the triage nurse went quickly, there were too many people there for the nurse to spend time interrogating her but sent her immediately into the ward where another nurse cleaned the wound and began stitching it after injecting the anaesthetic.

"How did it happen?" the nurse asked as she bound the arm.

"I was doing some carving," said Lisa. "I was working on a block of wood and the knife slipped."

"You were lucky. That could have got a lot deeper." The nurse was professionally detached, and Lisa departed half an hour later, her sleeve rolled down to hide the bandage. Not once did her parents notice anything and Lisa was determined to keep it that way.

* * *

"Now you are fulfilling your destiny," said the image of Anna Vulci.

"How?" muttered Lisa. She was mentally and physically exhausted from the killing of General Adams. The insane, raging hatred she had felt for the frail old man was quite incomprehensible to her, though the process of killing raised her to a high well above the previous murderous episodes.

"Have you thought about why you felt such rage when you saw the General?"

"Yes, I have. I wondered if perhaps he looked like somebody I disliked when I was younger."

Vulci smiled.

"That would not be enough. No, it is simple. The General was in a long line of descendants scattered around the world. He was a Tarquinian."

"A Tarquinian? And somehow I recognised it?"

"That's the result of wearing all three items cursed by the demon. Now you have the power to recognise the enemy."

"The enemy? But how could he be the enemy?"

"That's the final key to your powers that I must now tell you, Lisa."

"What's that?"

"You are a Vulci, Lisa."

Lisa felt she could take no further hammer blows that day.

Chapter 12 - The Homicide Squad

"We've got nothing. This is insane." Detective Inspector Adrian Cooper was more than irritated, he was furious.

"Possibly something, but very little," replied Mary Stanton. "Five knifing murders and still not a clue that we can use. The only thing we still know is that it's the same knife each time, the domestic carving knife with an eighteen centimetres long blade, three centimetres wide, only one cutting edge."

"The same knife each time," said Cooper. "Does that tell us anything?"

"It's sure as hell not a professional gang war," said Stanton. "It's weird, the fact that they only use one weapon indicates a bunch of amateurs, but the ability to hide all clues at the scene of crime says something else."

"But the pathologists did find something that could be very useful," said Detective Sergeant James Brigham.

Cooper and Mary exchanged glances and maintained straight faces.

"He speaks," exclaimed Cooper.

"It has been known," said Mary.

"Okay, James, what's the information?" asked Cooper.

"The General was holding a bayonet in his right hand and there was some blood on it," said Brigham.

"A bayonet? What, a good old "fix bayonets" thing at the end of a rifle?"

"The very same."

"And the blood?"

"The pathologist promised to bring their analysis here as soon as possible. In fact, that looks like him now."

As Brigham spoke, a young man entered the room. He greeted Mary as an old friend, then introduced himself to Cooper. "G'day, Inspector, Nick Bellamy, pathologist."

"Anything interesting?" asked Cooper.

"Probably, but not all that informative. We have no DNA match to anyone known to the police. SOCO also found three drops of blood on the carpet by the armchair where the General was sitting, and they match the blood on the bayonet. So it's likely that the General scored a hit on the attacker in front of him, while a second individual behind him slit his throat."

"But no identity?"

The pathologist shook his head. "That's all I can give you." With a wave, he left the office.

"You two know each other?" asked Cooper of Mary.

"We dated for a while a couple of years ago," she replied. "Nice bloke, highly intelligent, but never got the juices flowing."

"Too much information," said Cooper. "What about motive? Anything there?"

Mary shook her head. "The general's will left half

his estate to his granddaughter, but she's quite affluent already, runs a business selling batik cloth from Indonesia and Malaysia, does very well. And her husband is an investment banker, bloody rich. There's no motive there, unless there's some old family stress we don't know about. The other half went to a servicemen's charity. Jenny Symonds had nothing of value. She did own the cottage, but her only income is from her pension. Her solicitor will handle the sale of the cottage, and he has the address of a granddaughter living in Wales. She's in her sixties and not well, so hardly a suspect."

"So nothing new," said Cooper.

"But we have got something from the house to house." Mary Stanton looked at her notebook. "The women who lives in the house about a hundred metres away from Jenny Simonds' home said she saw a girl walking along the path behind the houses in that street two nights before the killing."

"Any description?" Cooper asked.

"Nothing useful," replied Stanton. "She said she only noticed her because it was unusual to see anybody on that path. But she did say the girl was perhaps fifteen or sixteen, definitely young, dressed in jeans and a black shirt. That's all. It was getting dark at that time."

"Well, it's something, I suppose," said Cooper. "What can we tell from the victims? There's something non-standard going on here. Any thoughts?"

"They're developing the skills," said Mary. "They started with the easiest possible victims, homeless derelicts in a slum region. Then old Jenny Simonds in her home. Slightly more complex, needing a bit more planning. Last of all, so far, the general. Now, that took serious planning and was a high-risk operation. Looks to me like they're tackling progressively harder targets."

Cooper nodded. "Makes sense," he said. "But Holy Christ, are they still planning? What in God's name do they move to next? He looked thoughtful. "Is there any link at all between the general and old Jenny Simonds?"

"Nothing that the postmortems revealed," said Stanton. "Jenny's ancestry is mostly Welsh, according to her DNA, her husband died six years ago."

"What about him? Cooper showed some interest. "What if we exhumed him and checked his DNA? James?'"

Brigham shook his head. "No need. His DNA was taken during the autopsy as a routine. Then he was cremated and his ashes scattered in the river."

"Anything from the DNA?" asked Cooper.

"Nothing unusual," said Brigham. "Apparently there was a trace of Northern Italy, but very slight. Other than that, pure Anglo-Saxon."

"There's no way we can identify that girl," said Stanton. "The witness at Jenny's place said maybe fifteen or so, but in the dusk, she could be anything from twelve to thirty."

"Is it worth going to the path and looking for footprints?" asked Cooper

"Negative," said Mary. "Heavy rain for two nights after the killing."

"Fuck," said Cooper. "There's nothing we can do to move the case along. We're getting some flak from the papers and tv. James, you talked to the media. Anything there?"

"Public Relations is putting out the usual stuff about all lines of investigation being followed and some leads being found, but I doubt anyone believes them." Brigham seemed irritated."

"Then all we can do is keep looking," said Cooper. "The odds are pretty good that there'll be another murder. Maybe they'll make a mistake this time."

Mary suddenly shook her head in annoyance.

"Something I just remembered, sorry sir, I should have raised this before, but I got some information through the usual police channels yesterday. I don't think it helps us, or even if it's relevant."

Cooper was irritated. "Okay, Constable, out with it."

"The day after the general was killed, there was an unexplained death in Carlyle, a man working for the local council, just dropped dead as he walked home in the evening. No suspicious elements found, no motive for a possible murder could be established, nobody seems to have benefitted from the death, but the DNA taken in the postmortem showed something. Just like the general, his ancestry goes back several generations to Northern Italy, possibly the region round Etruria."

"That's it?" Cooper's irritation didn't fade.

"Not quite, sir. There's a very similar report I saw in the Interpol files. A woman in Paris, an accountant in her thirties working for one of those humungous international accounting firms, dropped dead at her desk, roughly the same time as the bloke in Carlyle. She was in great health, apparently, a mother of three-year old twins, happily married. So a postmortem was taken, and DNA showed her ancestry going back over two thousand years to Northern Italy, just like the general."

"That's it?" said Cooper again.

"That's it, sir. I said it may not be relevant, but I found it a bit curious, the way two people in great health and with some common features in their DNA, both dropped dead at almost the same time."

"Lots of people all over Europe have ancestry going back to Italy," said Cooper. "Some historians say they descended from the Roman occupation. The timing is just coincidence."

"That probably explains it," said Mary. "I'll get back to work."

"Good idea," said Cooper. "Try and get James to pull his weight a bit, eh?" He smiled as he said it.

Chapter 13 – The Killing Lust Increases

Lisa went up to her room with a sense of urgency, and with accompanying vibrations of mixed fear and excitement in her body. Locking the door and placing a chair up against the door handle, she sat before the mirror, extracted the necklace, ring and bracelet and carefully put them on, one by one. As she did, she felt the rush of power to her body, mixed with an inexplicable surge of anger, though at what, she could not say.

She stared at the mirror as her image became the older, mature woman. For a moment, she was distracted by the sight of some tiny lines around the woman's mouth. Had she become older since the last time she had seen her, just a short time ago? She put aside that thought, looking for the image of the young woman she had become accustomed to seeing each time. She wasn't there.

"I am here with you," said a voice behind her. Heart thumping from the shock, Lisa turned her head and saw a woman standing by the wall. Trembling, she turned herself on her seat to face her. It was the woman whose image she had seen, but now there was a big difference. She was dressed in a short, pleated skirt, but it was unsuited to her heavy build. Her legs were encased in leather boots, and above her waist, her torso was encased in leather straps that hid her breasts. It was not an attractive image and quite frightening. There was menace in the woman's appearance.

Lisa's mouth was so dry, she couldn't form the words.

"Now that you have all three pieces, I can take form with you," said Vulci. "Nobody else will see me, but I will be here."

Lisa was still unable to speak.

"Let me tell you what is happening," said Vulci. "Those three items you are now wearing were all cursed by a demon, at the request of the Vulci family. The first, the necklace, raised the lust to kill, but it was not directed at anyone. When you added the ring, the power in you grew stronger, the ability and need to kill grew with it. But it was the bracelet that finished the process."

Lisa was able to form a few words.

"What process?" she said, her voice weak and rasping.

"Now you can recognise any Tarquinia," said Vulci. "Even those descended by hundreds of generations, if there is Tarquinian blood in them, you will recognise them and you will need to kill them."

"But there must be hundreds of them around the world," grated Lisa. "How can I do that?"

"You will find a way. And there is one more thing."

Lisa stared at her, uncomprehending.

"With the last item, you are now mine," said the strange woman. "I own you, I will always be with you, there is no escape for you."

Every emotion Lisa had been feeling was now replaced by just one. She was totally, dreadfully consumed by fear. For several minutes, Lisa sat, her hands on her face, trembling and whimpering. The wave slowly decreased, replaced by a growing sense of power and self-assurance. Finally, she looked up at Vulci.

"Have all the people I have killed so far been Tarquinian?"

"Not at all. You are a natural killer already, even at your age. The necklace enforced that, though you could not recognise it. But one of them was a justified killing."

"Which?"

"The general. His origins go right back to the early twelve families. His ancestors left Italy soon after the Romans had taken power. Some of them eventually came to the British lands. Deciding to kill him was the influence of the jewellery, though you would have killed him before the old lady, if he'd arrived at the school earlier."

"And must I now wait until I meet another Tarquinia before I kill again?"

Vulci smiled. "As I said, you are a natural killer, and your two supporters were always ready to follow a leader like you. You will select suitable victims in the near future."

Vulci snapped out of Lisa's vision, leaving her trembling and frightened. And yet, underneath the fear was exhilaration. Vulci had opened her mind to her true self.

She was a natural killer and there were plentiful targets for her. And she knew that she had to kill again, very soon.

* * *

It happened far quicker than she could have dreamed. Deciding not to involve Pete and Dylan, she gathered what she termed her "Killing Gear" and waited until her parents told her they both had late faculty meetings.

Taking the bus out to the slum area of town that was mostly abandoned buildings and the homes of so many derelicts, she entered one badly damaged house, donned her overalls, shoe covers, hood and mask and went walking round the area which was now dark. Hearing sounds of coughing from one house, she slowly entered, followed the sounds and to her delight, saw two old men sitting in the wrecks of armchairs.

It was all too easy. She walked up to the first man, who barely saw her until she was over him. She sliced the knife across his scrawny neck, and he fell backward in the chair, eyes staring at her. Quickly, she took the few paces to the second man, slammed the knife into his chest and watched with pleasure as blood spurted out onto her overalls. Turning back to the first victim, she could see no signs of life, but stabbed into his chest again and again, feeling almost erotic pleasure as the knife went in as far as the handle. Repeating the process with the second man, she finally stood for five minutes, looking at the scene she had created. Then with a grunt of satisfaction, she left.

"God, that was great," she muttered as he slipped out of her "Killing Gear," put the items back in the garbage bag and returned home before her parents got back. She knew that she had time the next day after getting back from school to put the overalls and shoe covers into the washing machine and set it to the heaviest laundry process she could.

* * *

Three days later, Lisa met the two boys in the place that had become a habit, a bench by the side of the playing field, while the school rugby team practiced for their weekend match against a school in the next town. It was good camouflage, as there was always a fair-sized crowd of students watching the practice. As usual, Jake was the main point of interest for the large numbers of girls in the crowd, which usually caused Lisa considerable pride.

Today, something was different. As Pete and Dylan talked incessantly, if softly about their experiences to date, Lisa stared at Jake, feeling a growing anger in herself.

"What the hell is going on?" she thought. *"Why the anger? I always feel pride and considerable sexual emotions, seeing my boyfriend being such a great athlete. What is this?"*

Barely hearing the soft chatter of the two boys, Lisa continued to watch Jake, the anger growing in her. As the whistle blew for a pause, Jake ran across the field to her.

"Oh-oh, the muscleman approaches," said Dylan. He and Pete had developed a serious antipathy to Jake, their jealousy growing as they felt their own powerful commitment to Lisa.

Lisa hardly heard them, As Jake approached, she heard a voice behind her. She didn't turn round, she knew who it was.

"He's Tarquinian," said Vulci.

Lisa saw the cause of her anger. She realised she had somehow recognised Jake's ancestry, even without wearing any of the Etruscan pieces, but had not understood what she had seen. Now she fully understood and knew what she had to do.

As Jake neared, she gently pulled up the hem of her skirt to reveal more of her legs and then crossed them. The effect on Pete and Dylan was strong and proved to her that this technique would work.

"Hi, Jake," she said in her most seductive voice. "You're looking really good out there."

Under the anger, she knew she had spoken the truth. Jake's excellent body and muscular legs under the white shorts had always excited her. It was easy to gear up the seduction.

"You're looking pretty gorgeous yourself, Lisa," he said, his eyes firmly on her well-displayed thighs.

She uncrossed her legs and switched them, revealing even more of her body.

Jake tore his gaze away to glare at the two boys. "Can't you two little twerps push off somewhere? Don't you have your dolls to play with?"

Lisa looked sideways briefly and gestured to Pete and Dylan to leave. They obeyed without hesitation. She turned her face back to Jake and smiled.

"You're right, Jake. I much prefer the company of a real man."

He sat down next to her and put his arm round her shoulder. She snuggled up to him and placed a hand on his thigh. She could sense his breath coming faster.

"Why don't we go out tonight?" she whispered, turning her face into his neck.

"You bet we will," he replied softly. "Where do you think?"

"I know the very place," she said. "We'll be able to enjoy ourselves properly."

In the middle of the field, the whistle blew to resume practice. Regretfully, Jake took his arm away and stood up. "I'll see you at our regular place at seven," he said.

"I can't wait," she whispered and blew him a kiss. He returned it, turned and ran back to the centre. Lisa walked back to the school building.

"I'm meeting him at seven, behind the supermarket," she said as the two boys walked up, dismay in their faces. "You go to where we met before we did the old lady. Jake and I will get there about half past seven.”

“What?” exclaimed Dylan. “Why? Won’t you want to concentrate on Mr Muscles there?”

“We all will,” she replied and watched as comprehension slowly dawned on their faces, followed by excitement.

“How will we do it?” asked Pete. “He’s a lot bigger than we are and very strong.”

“I’ll show you then,” she replied and walked down the corridor to the girls’ washroom.

* * *

“They’re coming,” muttered Pete.

“About time,” said Dylan. “I’m getting stiff as a board, hiding here.”

“Best place to be,” said Pete. “He won’t see us behind this bush.”

“He won’t see anything. Look at the skirt she’s wearing, and she’s unbuttoned her blouse.”

“Good grief.” Pete stirred uncomfortably. “I’ve never seen her like that.”

“Why is she carrying her shoes?” muttered Dylan.

Pete shook his head.

They fell silent as Jake and Lisa neared, arms round each other’s waists.

“Let’s sit here,” said Lisa. She pointed at the short wall that ran along the track, it was just about seating height and the two settled down comfortably. They were a few steps from where the two boys were hiding.

Lisa snuggled even closer to Jake and moaned in pleasure as his other hand shifted to her breasts. But she moved the hand she'd placed on his neck and waved minutely.

Dylan took the weapon she'd given him a few days earlier. It was a length of piano wire with a wooden handle at each end. He nodded at Pete, and they slowly eased their way from behind the bush and up to the other two who were fully engaged in their activity.

Standing behind Jake, Dylan slipped the garotte over Jake's head, down to his neck and pulled hard, placing his knee against Jake's shoulder. Jake struggled furiously, but he was prevented from anything effective as Pete slipped down in front of him, seized his legs and clung on tight. Lisa stood up and moved away. Although Jake's arms were free, he was desperately trying to move the garotte from his neck.

Dylan pulled harder and felt the wire cut through Jake's neck, blood spurting out all down his body as he went still. He released the wire and lifted it back over Jake's head.

"Well done," said Lisa, coming closer. "I had to stand away, couldn't risk any of his blood on my clothes."

The two boys were unable to speak. Both were staring at her breasts that had come free during the clinch with Jake. And her skirt was well up to her waist.

Realising the situation, Lisa turned away, buttoning up her blouse and pulling the skirt down over her thighs.

"Right," she said. "Now we have to move him into the bushes, well away from the path. Not many people come here, it could be days before anyone finds him, even after he's been reported as missing. Come on, hurry, you'll have to do it, I could get blood on me."

Obediently, Pete and Dylan lifted Jake and carried him a few metres into the wood. Dropping him in a ditch under large bushes, they walked back to Lisa, who was wearing a raincoat.

"How did...?" gasped Dylan.

"I hid that near here a couple of days ago," she replied. "I knew I'd need it someday. This way, I won't be so obvious as I go home. You two, get those overalls and foot covers off and put the garotte in the bag also. Throw that in the river when you get a chance and make sure you wash the overalls thoroughly."

An hour later, all three were at home.

Chapter 14 – The Homicide Squad

"I tell you what, Guv, this case is getting curiouser and curiouser," said Detective Senior Constable Mary Stanton. She was wearing her usual pants-suit that fitted her tall frame well, and her reddish-brown hair was tied in a ponytail. The two men looked at her with appreciation.

"Are you now the Red Queen?" asked the Inspector. "What's getting curiouser and curiouser?"

Detective Sergeant James Brigham looked amused. "What the hell are you two talking about? Who's the Red Queen?"

"Have you never read *'Alice in Wonderland'?*" said Stanton.

"No," replied Brigham. "What's it got to with this case?"

"Alice falls down a rabbit hole and finds herself at the Mad Hatter's Tea Party." Detective Inspector Cooper showed no expression. "Also there was the Red Queen, who claimed that she could think of six impossible things before breakfast."

"I don't get it," said Brigham.

"I feel we're at that party," said Mary Stanton. "This case is crazy, and several impossible things are happening."

"Fill us in," said Cooper.

Stanton opened her case book.

"We had three old derelicts killed on two separate nights, several days apart," she began. "A few days later, we had the murder of the old lady, no motive for any of these. The General was killed in his own home, shortly after, same method as the old lady, no motive can be detected. A week ago, two more old derelicts were killed in the same area as before, the abandoned housing estate. All of those were killed by what seems to be the same weapon, a domestic kitchen knife and there was not a trace of evidence to point to a killer at any of the murder sites, other than the blood on the general's bayonet and the drops of the same blood on the carpet. But those traces have given us nothing."

"And that is almost certainly an impossible thing," said Cooper. "Seven killings, more than enough to name this the work of a serial killer following the same modus operandi, not a trace of evidence. I can't think of even a remotely similar case in the UK before."

"I can," said Mary. "Once I saw the number of murders, I did a search. You'd be amazed at how many serial killers we've had over the years."

"As many as these?" asked Cooper.

"A lot," replied Mary. "But the worst has to be Doctor Harold Shipman. Remember him?"

"Oh hell, yes," said Cooper. "Known as "Doctor Death," an actual doctor who killed over two hundred patients in his care."

"Could have been over two hundred and fifty," added Brigham. "I remember reading about him."

"And then there was Peter Sutcliffe, called 'The Yorkshire Ripper,'" added Mary. "Murdered at least thirteen women in Yorkshire and Manchester."

"Alright, you've corrected me," said Cooper. "This is not the worst we've seen. Bad enough though, and we're not getting anywhere."

"And now this young man, Jake Cahill, bringing the total to eight," continued Mary Stanton. "A completely different modus operandi with a different weapon. The style of the wound suggests a garotte, according to the experts. Who the hell uses a garotte?"

"It was popular in wartime for commandoes and such, but I've not heard of one being used in many years," said Cooper.

"And although we still don't have footprints, we do now have signs that said there were at least three people involved," continued Mary. "The grass behind the wall where Jake was apparently killed was seriously disturbed by two individuals wearing foot coverings. Then his body was carried to where it was dumped in a ditch about fifty metres away. He was a big lad, it would have taken at least two people to carry him, and the traces of feet to the ditch also showed two people involved. This time, we have something. There were prints of a naked foot, almost certainly female in the same crime scene. Looks like Jake had a girl with him."

"Can the scene of crime officer estimate the size of the feet?"

Stanton shook her head. "It was too grassy," she said. "We could only get indications of toes, hence the naked conclusion, but not the size."

Cooper looked at the Sergeant.

"Anything from your work, James?"

"We've been interviewing many of the kids at the school," said Brigham. "It seems Jake was extremely popular, especially with the girls."

"Not surprising," said Mary. "He was a good-looking young man, highly athletic and the captain of the school Rugby team."

"But oddly, despite being just seventeen, he apparently had a relationship with a girl in Grade Seven, Lisa Kendricks, fourteen years old," added Brigham.

"Fourteen? Good grief. Has anyone talked to her, yet?" asked Cooper.

Brigham shook his head. "She's been away from school since the murder."

"Okay, next priority, you two go and talk to her at her house," said Cooper. "Make sure you call her parents first and have at least one responsible adult there."

"Yes, Guv," said Brigham.

"But Guv, there's one more thing," said Stanton. "And this is what's making this like the Mad Hatter's Tea Party."

"Explain," said Cooper.

"As you know, the DNA taken from the General

showed ancestry going back to Northern Italy. Two days after his murder, there were two unexplained deaths, one in Carlyle, one in Paris, two healthy people who just dropped dead. I got the DNA readings from the postmortem from the local cops in Carlyle, the Interpol files showed the DNA from that death, both showed ancestry going back to Northern Italy."

"Yes, and as I said, that's not so unusual, thousands of people moved all over Europe during the Roman Empire days." Cooper seemed interested, despite his comment.

"True, Guv, but here's the thing. Jake Cahill's DNA was also taken and it too showed ancestry going back to Northern Italy."

"Okay, a little bit curiouser," said Cooper, showing considerable attention to her.

"Now hang on to your hat," said Mary. "I circulated flags through Interpol and the UK cops, and I got two responses. There was a sudden, unexplained death in Oslo the day after Jake was killed. A young woman, a fitness instructor, dropped dead at her gym. The postmortem showed no possible reason, she was in perfect health. But her DNA showed ancestry going back to Northern Italy."

Cooper showed no reaction beyond a tightening of his hands on the desk.

"And the final impossible thing," continued Mary. "The mayor of a small town in Croatia died while running a town council meeting, the morning after

Jake's death. No warning, he just slumped. Nothing shown in the postmortem, but, you guessed it, Northern Italy ancestry. In fact, I checked the times. Both those two deaths occurred within minutes of each other."

"And curiouser,' said Cooper.

"What the hell is going on?" Brigham was angry. "How can these simultaneous unexplained deaths have anything to do with our serial killer here?"

"Better go and talk to this Lisa Kendricks," said Cooper.

* * *

"Mrs Kendricks, thank you for giving us your time," said Brigham. "As you know, we must have a responsible adult present when interviewing a child."

Mary Stanton sat back to watch her colleague at work. When out of the office, Brigham was a highly competent officer with a probing interview style and Mary had no difficulty with her superior taking charge.

"That's *Doctor* Kendricks." Lisa's mother was clearly annoyed. "And why do you need to interview Lisa? She can't have anything to do with this horrible event."

"Doctor Kendricks, our apologies." Mary Stanton showed contrition, and it seemed to reduce the tension in the room. "But it was reported by several students that Lisa had a fairly close relationship with Jake Cahill, even that they dated. So you can see, we have to talk to her."

"Dated? What could you possibly mean, Constable Stanton? She's fourteen, for God's sake, the boy was seventeen."

"I'm reporting what we heard, Doctor Kendricks," said Mary.

The woman turned to stare at Lisa, who had been silently sitting in an armchair in the Kendricks house since the detectives had entered.

"Lisa, tell them this is nonsense," she said loudly. "Did you even know this boy?"

For a few seconds, Lisa felt intimidated before the anger in her mother. She had always felt that way with her, almost crushed by the authoritativeness and commanding presence. With her father, she had no problems, he was a gentle man who obviously adored his only child.

But as she looked up at her mother, she felt confidence filling her, almost a sense of power, rather like the sensation when she put on the jewellery she kept hidden in her room.

"No, Mum," she said, looking her mother directly in the eye. "I knew him, of course, but we didn't date. But I liked talking to him sometimes, he didn't treat me like a silly little girl, the way some of the older boys do."

She saw uncertainty in her mother's face, something she had never seen before. She tried not to smile as her mother sat down in a chair by the wall.

Mary took over, as she and Brigham had previously agreed, thinking that Lisa might respond more easily to a woman.

"So, Lisa, you confirm that you had no relationship with Jake Cahill, other than occasional talks?"

"That's correct, Constable Stanton." Lisa felt her confidence growing further as she saw that the detective seemed uncomfortable.

"Can you think of anyone who might want to kill him?"

"A few of the boys at school, perhaps."

"Why would they feel that, Lisa?"

"Jealousy, Constable. Jake was the school hero, he captained the rugby team and the cricket team, he was on the school teams for athletics and basketball, and he was seriously gorgeous, a real hunk. He could have had any girl in the school."

"Even you, Lisa?"

Lisa laughed. "I'm fourteen, Constable, he was seventeen."

Mary consulted her notes. "We also have reports that you were friends with Franklin and Dylan Marlow, who were in the same class as you."

"Those two losers?" Lisa snorted her contempt. "They're nobodies, they've got no friends, they can't do any sports. So I'm being nice to them. I know I'm popular, so talking to them now and again is just something I can do to help them."

"I'm sure they're grateful," said Mary, beginning to

feel a strong dislike for the girl. "Back to Jake. Where were you the night he was killed?"

"I was at the movies. I went to see Barbie."

"I can confirm she was out that evening." Doctor Kendricks spoke up from the side of the room.

"Thank you, Doctor," said Mary. "Lisa, we know there was a girl with Jake about the time he was killed. do you know who that was?"

"Why should I? I don't keep tabs on every boy in the school."

Mary decided she'd had enough. She looked up at Brigham and saw his small shake of the head. She folded up her case book and replaced it in her handbag, stood up and within minutes, they were outside the house and back in Brigham's car.

"Shit," exclaimed Mary. "If she's fourteen, I'm the queen of Sheba."

"Fourteen, going on thirty," said Brigham. "I'm glad we agreed that you should interview her. I could never have coped. Girls weren't like that when I was that age."

"Definitely mature," agreed Mary. "She had the curves of somebody several years older, and composure I've never seen in anyone of her age."

"Being questioned by a homicide detective, and she's as cool as a cucumber? Absolutely."

Mary laughed. "Fancy a drink? I need one after all that raging femininity."

"Thought you'd never ask," said Brigham.

Chapter 15 – The End of the Etruscans

280 BCE, Etruria

The House of Vulci was in huge distress and grief. A messenger from the battle had arrived with the news that had been feared for years since the war against Rome had started fifteen years before.

The head of the Vulci House raised his face with tears pouring down.

"The damned Romans have taken the coast," sobbed Thucer. "They have blocked our army from getting help from others of the Twelve Family forces and they are now advancing inland. We may have only days."

His daughter, Ramutha crouched on a pile of rugs was weeping heavily but raised her face to look at him.

"Father, what can we do?" Her voice was broken by the tears in her throat.

"We must prepare," replied Thucer. "Let all the servants and the slaves go, they must take their chances away from this house. Let them take anything they want, we cannot use them again."

"Father, this is not the way of the Twelve," shouted Thefarie. Although not yet twenty years old, his son stood straight and proud, his hand on his sword hanging from his belt. "We are the rulers of this land, how can we surrender to this mob of hooligans that call themselves Romans? We were far greater than Rome for centuries, there is no need to bow down to them now."

Thucer looked sadly at his son. "You are right, we of Etruria ruled most of this land and other lands across the oceans for over a thousand years. The House of Vulci has been a leader of the Twelve Families that ruled our nation with wisdom and strength. But our time has ended. The Romans have been growing in power for three centuries and now we must accept that it is their time."

He turned and looked round the dozen people assembled in the room, then turned back to his son.

"Thefarie, take the duties of the head of the household. Go down to the servants' quarters and tell them what I said before. They must now leave, take what they want and give them the blessings of the gods that they will survive as citizens of this Roman country."

Thefarie stood rigid for a few moments, almost ready to defy his father, then walked out of the room. There was a mutual gasp of relief from the others, who had witnessed Thefarie's anger and violence when thwarted in the past.

"And now we ourselves must prepare," said Thucer. "We have little time left."

The sounds of a large body of armed men woke the family soon after dawn. Rising from their beds was difficult for all of them, accustomed as they were to the help of a servant or slave, but the fear drove all of them to dress hurriedly.

Heavy banging on the door reverberated through the house. Thucer Vulci took a deep breath and opened the heavy wooden door. It swung slowly with a squeal of unoiled hinges.

Standing in front of Thucer was a Roman soldier. He was tall, taller even than Thucer's son, and the pride and confidence in his stance almost radiated. Behind him stood the men of what Thucer could see was a Century, the standard unit of a hundred soldiers.

"I am Centurian Clemens Annius," said the man before Thucer. "I have orders to take over this house as the headquarters of this battalion and its commanding officers. You will leave immediately."

"Are all members of this family being ordered away?" asked Thucer, struggling to stop the despair from overwhelming him.

"Only the leaders," replied the Centurian. "But I can tell you that the same is true of all the Twelve Families. The leaders are being ordered out of the country. We Romans must have no enemies within."

"May we at least pack our essentials?" asked Thucer. "And may we take our horses and carriages? There are twelve of us."

Just for a few seconds, the Centurian's face showed some pity.

"You may. You have until the sun is at its highest."

Thucer closed the door and turned back to his family standing in the hallway.

"Where will we go, Father?" asked Ramutha. Her hair was tangled, uncombed, missing the work of her personal servant who had left two days before.

"We head north and west," said Thucer. "There are countries in those regions who may look kindly on us. We ruled them once, but we were not harsh rulers. Now that our positions are reversed, we may have a chance at a life."

"We will probably find others of the Twelve as we travel," said Thefarie.

"Very possible," agreed Thucer. "But you must not carry on the warfare between us and the Tarquinia, should we encounter them. The time for killing is past. All of us are now homeless, let peace prevail."

Thefarie looked angry for a moment until his father's words sunk in.

"Let's go and find a new home," he said.

Chapter 16 – England

Detective Senior Constable Mary Stanton did not have the luxury of an office, normally having only a desk in the open plan area of the police station. But today, she had the use of her colleague's office, that of Detective Sergeant Brigham who was attending a refresher course at the shooting range. The private space proved to be useful when she got a call from the front desk sergeant.

"Mary, there's a bloke here to see you. Says he's Nick Bellamy from the pathologist's office."

"Oh," said Mary in some surprise. "Thanks, Sergeant, send him in. I'm in Brigham's office today."

A few moments later, the slender frame of her ex-boyfriend appeared. She waved him to a chair across from the desk. "Nick, what brings you here? Are you back to lusting for my gorgeous body?"

He laughed. Their one-time romance had morphed into a warm friendship without sexual content. "Nah," he said. "I ran out of Viagara a while ago. But I do have something that might interest you." He pulled a sheet of paper from his briefcase.

"About this current case, the murder of the General?"

"Much wider than that. I read your reports about this series of murders and how you had picked up on some unexplained deaths in England and in Europe and this whole Northern Italy thing."

"You've found something?" Mary felt a rush of interest.

"I have. It triggered my curiosity. I got my boss to talk to some high-up cops in the Metropolitan Police, and they contacted people in Interpol, and they were able to get the full pathology reports on those curious deaths. The Europeans have been adopting some advanced DNA research techniques, and they used that to identify uniparental markers in the DNA."

"Uniparental?"

"They're into autosomal analysis, so both Y-DNA which shows the male connections and what they call mtDNA which provides the maternal links. That would probably have helped trace the families, but we went one better. I asked my boss to contact the University which had led the archaeological investigations of those Etruscan tombs and ask them if they would take DNA samples from bodies in those tombs. They agreed and said they'd take samples from teeth, which keep the DNA very well. We got those results a few days ago. So now they can identify the actual family links in the DNA."

Mary sat up straight. "And what did they find?

"Every one of those sudden deaths came from people from a single-family path, the Vulci, going back to Northern Italy."

"Nick, that's impossible, surely? How can people from all over Europe have been descended from a single family?"

"The traces were very tiny, as obviously there were many families involved through breeding outside of that line, but these days we can track it."

"Good grief," said Mary.

"Ah, but that's not all," said Nick. "Now it gets curiouser and curiouser." He smiled at the excitement in Mary's face. "As you have already learnt, two of the victims in your case have also shown an ancestry going back to Northern Italy."

"Not part of the same family, surely?"

He shook his head. "Not the same family as those sudden deaths, no. But they were the same as each other. The General and that young man Jake, they did come from the same family line, the Tarquinia."

Mary let out a long breath, not realising she'd been holding it.

"Holy clucking duckshit," she said.

"My words exactly," replied Nick. "And now the hammer blow," he continued. "Not just curiouser, but downright bloody impossible. I checked the times of these deaths. They all occurred in working hours, with people around them, so the time they collapsed is recorded. The man who dropped dead in Carlyle and the woman who died in Paris, both occurred at exactly the same time and just sixteen hours after the General was murdered. And again, the woman who died in Oslo and the man in Croatia also died at exactly the same time, fourteen hours after Jake was killed."

Mary was struggling for breath.

"You're right, downright bloody impossible. Actually, I'd already checked the times of those last two deaths and was a bit gobsmacked by it, but I didn't know about the others. There are no weird stories relating to the deaths of the derelicts and the old lady?"

Nick shook his head. "Nothing. As your notes from your meetings with Cooper and Brigham suggest, those killings seem to be practice runs for more advanced operations."

"But this is horrible, Nick. Something quite incomprehensible is going on, but there's no way we can prove those sudden deaths are in any way linked to the serial killings we're getting here."

"I agree, it's spooky as hell, almost Black Magic. There's no bloody way any killer could organise these events like that, especially as we have no idea how or why those four people died."

"Do you have all this documented?"

"Naturally. This copy is for you."

Mary took a few moments to control her breathing, then picked up the phone.

"Sir, Mary Stanton here. I have some very strange data from the pathologist. Can I come and see you?"

She looked at Nick.

"I owe you at least a lunch for this," she said. "But it will have to be later. My boss said to come over right away."

"Then I shall mourn bitterly for the lack of your company," said Nick. "But I understand the ways of the police." He stood up and turned to the door.

"Yah booh," said Mary.

Chapter 17 – England

Lisa slowly donned all three jewellery items and watched her face in the mirror as the image aged to that of a woman in her twenties.

"There must be a change for you now," said a voice behind her. Lisa looked in the mirror and saw Vulci standing in the room. This time, she was dressed in conventional modern clothing, a simple grey pants suit, her long hair tied in a ponytail. The face was not attractive.

"What sort of change?" asked Lisa.

"There were the only two of the Tarquinia line in the country," said Vulci. "And you have killed them both. For now, you cannot continue."

"Can't I continue with others who are not of the line? I need to kill, it's essential for me."

"Lisa, so far, I have protected you from excess curiosity. I have ensured that the police have not yet established absolute links between you and the killings."

"How have you done that? And are there such links?"

"I assure you, without my placing some blocks in their minds, they would by now be certain that you are complicit in these killings. That would prevent you fulfilling your destiny any further."

"So what must I do?"

"You must commit two more killings. There are only those two witnesses to your actions."

"Dylan and Pete? I must kill them?"

"They are the only ones who can definitely incriminate you. You cannot take the chance."

"I understand," Lisa said. She felt no pity for the two boys, no regrets that they had to die, only a logical understanding of what Vulci had said. "And what happens after that? You said I can't continue. Does that mean it all stops here?"

"It's temporary. For you to find and kill more Tarquinia, you must travel in Europe where almost all the Etruscan families settled. There may be others elsewhere in the world, but those in Europe can keep you occupied for some years. But for that, you must be able to leave home and travel as an adult."

"I can't afford to travel alone for some years. How can I do this?"

"I have the solution. But I will give it to you when the time is right. Now, start planning for your removal of your witnesses."

"I will," said Lisa, her mind already thinking of the approach she would take.

* * *

"I wish she'd hurry up," said Dylan. He and Pete were already dressed in their protective gear, including the covering for their feet. They had donned these back in the old alleyway they had met with Lisa for the killing of the old tramp.

"Did she say who the target was tonight?" Pete was irritable, feeling the cold of the night air and anxious to get the job done.

"She didn't. Ah, here she is," said Dylan as Lisa appeared on the footpath to where the two boys were waiting in the dense bushes. She was also wearing the full protective clothing

"Lisa, who are we doing tonight?" asked Pete.

"Tell you in a moment," she replied. "Now, have you both got weapons now? I want you to be the primary killers this time, you deserve it."

"Great," exclaimed Pete. "Yes, I've got a large box-cutter, the same as Dylan has."

"Let's see them both," said Lisa and watched as both boys produced the heavy cutters.

"Open them up," commanded Lisa. "Dylan, let's see yours. Are you sure it's as sharp as possible?"

"Damn sure," he replied. "I sharpened it yesterday when you called to say get ready."

"Pete?" she asked.

"The same," replied Pete and showed her his blade, the cutting metal fully extracted.

"Let me see," said Lisa.

As Pete handed over the cutter, she pretended to examine it, then in a sudden, rapid swing, sliced the blade across Pete's throat. Blood gushed from the wound, over the knife, her hand in its glove and down Pete's chest. His eyes showed terror as he gasped for breath.

"Lisa, what the hell?" screamed Dylan and turned and began to run. He didn't get far in the long grass. He tripped and fell forward. Lisa had followed him immediately, she leaped on his back, pulled his head back with one hand in his hair and sliced his throat in one smooth motion. Dylan's face fell back into the grass, his body shook for a few seconds, then went still.

Lisa stood up and walked back to where Pete lay outstretched, obviously dead.

"Sorry, guys," she said. "You were well past your use by date."

She dropped the cutter by Dylan's body and walked away without a second look.

* * *

"Looks like Pete tried to run away when Dylan threatened him with his weapon, Dylan followed him, killed him and then committed suicide with Pete's weapon," said Detective Inspector Cooper.

"Doesn't make real sense," said Detective Sergeant Brigham. "Pete was killed with his own knife, and then Dylan comes back with it and kills himself."

"Yeah well, that's how it looks to me," said Cooper. His face registered puzzlement. "Not quite why..." He stopped.

"I suppose so," said Brigham. He sounded reluctant but was unable to express the reason.

"Yeah, it's not quite..." muttered Mary Stanton and stopped. "That will be the report to the Coroner?"

"It will," said Cooper. "Those kids did the other killings, case closed."

"I'm still not..." said Mary.

"Not what?" demanded Cooper. "You questioning my judgement, Constable?"

Mary shook her head. "No sir, I can't. That does look like the answer to all the killings."

"Good," said Cooper. "Case closed Let's get back to the other problems we have. Fancy a drink in the pub to celebrate?"

* * *

"They should have addressed the issue of why the two boys had been seen talking to you many times," said Vulci. "But I clouded their minds enough so that nobody knew of that connection. You're not under suspicion. The case is closed, and the coroner will accept that finding."

"But how did you do that?" Lisa began to query the powers of Vulci. "I thought you were just the ghost of a long-dead Vulci. How does a ghost get the sort of powers you have to affect people's minds?"

The image smiled at her. "Perhaps I have not been entirely truthful, Lisa."

Lisa felt a cold shiver run through her. Something frightening was happening.

"I am not the ghost of a long-dead Vulci," continued the image. "I am the demon that laid the curse on the Tarquinia at the command of the Vulci, twenty-five hundred years ago. But even that is not the full story. Look at me."

The image of a middle-aged woman in a pants suit changed. Now she was back as Lisa had first seen her, a heavy-set woman in a short, pleated skirt, her breasts bound with leather straps, knee-length boots and carrying a huge hammer. It was a frightening sight, there was so much menace in it.

"My name is Vanth," said the woman. "Some called me the Angel of Death, but my main task was to lead the newly dead into the underworld. I have shepherded many into that dark place."

Lisa drew in her breath in shock. She said nothing, the fear freezing her tongue.

"It changes nothing," said the demon. "Your path is fixed, I will continue to help you follow it."

It took her several moments before Lisa could speak again. "So now what?" she said.

"Now, Lisa, you put the three pieces back in that drawer, lock it and leave them there until the time is right."

"How will I know?" Lisa asked, the fear diminishing as she realised the demon would help her do what she most desired to do, kill Tarquinia.

"You will know." Vulci vanished.

Regretfully, Lisa did as instructed, wondering when that exciting time would return.

Chapter 18

Lisa was halfway down the stairs when she heard the raised, angry voices of her parents. This had never happened before. She stopped and sat down on the stairs.

"I'm married to a bad-tempered, ignorant bigot," shouted her father. "It's never been any fun, I assure you."

"You didn't have to marry me," her mother replied, the volume making her voice easily audible to Lisa. "I sure as hell didn't want to. You're nothing but a low-grade academic, no money, no class."

"You know bloody well why we got married. Your stinking rich family demanded it when you got pregnant and told them you were getting an abortion. Your father threatened me with total ruin if I didn't marry you, and he had the power do that."

"And I damn well should have got that abortion," screamed her mother. "I just knew the girl was evil, I could tell even after three months. And obviously I was right, she sure as hell is evil."

"What the hell are you talking about?"

"You know what I'm talking about, you fool. Who the hell is doing all these killings around here? Your fucking daughter, that's who. Haven't you noticed she's always been out late when any of those people were killed? And I found the overalls she bought when she left them in the washing machine one day. There were still signs of blood on them."

Oh my god, she knows? Lisa was shaken. *How the hell does she know? This has to be stopped.*

"You're lying," shouted the professor. "What bloody nonsense, a fourteen-year-old girl responsible for killing people? You're quite mad, you stupid bitch."

"No, you're the stupid one, supposed to be a brilliant academic and you can't put two and two together where it's your daughter concerned. She's a serial killer and I'm going to tell the police."

"Like hell you are." Lisa could hear the anger in her father's voice.

There was a scream of fear from her mother, then some odd gargling noises, followed by silence. Lisa ran down the stairs and opened the door to the lounge. Her father was bent over her mother's body, slumped over an armchair, his hands still on the woman's throat.

Kendricks released the body and stood up, turning to Lisa. He looked dazed.

"I'm sorry, Lisa," he mumbled. "I had to do it."

Feeling astonishing calm, Lisa touched her father on his arm.

"I know Dad," she said. "I understand." *Well, if he hadn't done it, I would have had to.*

"I couldn't let her do it," he said. "I couldn't let her hurt you."

"I know Dad, I understand," she said again. "Let's get her into the shed."

Still looking dazed and uncomprehending, her father followed Lisa's lead, and they carried the body of her mother out to the garden shed, laying her down on the ground. Kendricks bent over the body, tears starting to rise on his face. Behind him, Lisa looked around, picked up a hammer from the shelf and struck hard on her father's head. He collapsed immediately, without a sound and Lisa knew he was dead.

"Sorry, Dad," she said softly. "But you knew she was right. I couldn't risk you telling."

She wiped the handle of the hammer down with an oily rag lying on the bench and returned to the house. She went back up to her room and played a computer game for over ninety minutes, then went back down, picked up the telephone and dialled the 999 emergency code. When a voice answered, Lisa screamed into it, putting on the most panicked sound she could.

"Please come," she called. "My parents are dead."

The calming voice at the other end asked for details and the address. When she replaced the phone, Lisa smiled.

"That was an Oscar-winning performance," she told herself and sat down in the armchair that had held her mother's body. When she heard the sounds of police sirens approaching, she went into the kitchen, threw water all over her face and adopted a grief-stricken look. Then she went to the front door and opened it as two cars stopped by the front gate.

* * *

"It looks like a simple intrusion," said Detective Inspector Cooper. "The back door to the house was open, so no break-in was needed, it looks like the killer saw Mrs Kendricks in the garden shed and killed her there before going into the house, but Mr Kendricks must have seen him from inside the house, went to the shed, found his wife and bent over her. The killer must have been hiding, then hit Mr Kendricks with the large hammer on the tool rack. The pathologist says the single blow would have caused instant death."

"And the killer was wearing gloves," said Mary Stanton. "No fingerprints on the hammer."

"Exactly," said Cooper. "Lisa was working in her bedroom, came down later and saw the door open, went to the shed and found that appalling scene."

"Apparently ninety minutes after the killing," said Brigham. "That agrees with the pathologist's report that death occurred between one and two hours earlier."

"What a dreadful thing for a child to find," said Mary. "But I must say, she's displayed amazing composure."

"Maybe too much," said Mary Stanton.

The other two looked at her.

"Explain," said Cooper.

"Lisa seems to have been involved with a significant number of these deaths," said Mary. "She was the boyfriend of Jake, she was pally with the two boys, and now her parents. It smells a bit to me."

"God almighty, you think a girl of fourteen could be involved in five murders, all within the last year?" Cooper looked shocked.

"Makes no sense, does it, Guv?" Mary's face was expressionless.

"God, I bloody well hope it doesn't," replied the Inspector. "A serial killer barely a teenager? That's too horrible to contemplate."

"It gives me nightmares," chimed in Brigham.

"I doubt we'll find the killer," said Cooper. "Looks like a simple opportunistic act, there are no clues, no prints, nothing."

"I imagine the coroner will return a verdict of "Murder by person or persons unknown," said Brigham.

"Can't see any other," said Cooper. "Despite what Mary is thinking."

* * *

"Lisa, let me offer my deepest sympathies," said Benjamin Hollier. "No child should lose their parents like that."

"Thank you, Mr Hollier." Lisa sat in one chair across from the solicitor, her aunt next to her.

"And so to details," said Hollier. "Lisa, you are now thirteen, I understand. Your aunt has agreed to take you for as long as needed at her home in Reading. Can I offer you, Mrs Grimshaw, my condolences for the loss of your sister?"

"Thank you," said the woman next to Lisa. "It's a terrible loss for the whole family. Our parents are most distressed."

"I'm sure," said Hollier. "Now, the final wills of both parents were opened. It is assumed that Mrs Kendricks died first, and her will leaves everything to her husband. His will specified the sole beneficiary as Lisa. So the financial sum of just under three million pounds, plus the house will be held in trust by the executor, that is Simon Kendricks, the brother of the deceased. Is that understood?"

"I don't like the idea of Simon managing the trust fund," said Grimshaw. "That entire family has always been poor, I can't trust any of them to be in charge of such a huge sum."

"You can lodge a complaint and objection," said Hollier. "But I must be frank, there will be few or no grounds for a successful appeal."

Grimshaw said nothing.

My God, she's as big a bitch as my mother, thought Lisa. *How the hell can I live with that awful family for five years? I'll just have to manage, thinking of that huge sum of money coming to me then. Maybe I can kill her as well. Anyway, it's a good thing that I'll be at another school. This one was getting difficult.* The thought comforted her, and she stayed silent and unmoving.

"The house will be rented and managed by a real estate agent, the proceeds being added to the trust fund, which will also handle expenses, such as maintenance, rates and insurance. When Lisa turns eighteen, the entire estate will be turned over to her."

He lifted his head from the documents and faced Lisa.

"However, Lisa, you will be legally able to live on your own on reaching the age of sixteen, so you may decide to reclaim the house and live there, receiving an allowance from the estate. Tell me if you decide this path and I will inform the estate agent."

Oh, that's better, thought Lisa. *Less than two years to survive with those awful people. I can manage that.*

Hollier turned back to the aunt.

"Until then, Mrs Grimshaw you have agreed to provide a home and support to Lisa and will receive an allowance from the trust, to be arranged between you and the executor. Are you both clear on that?"

Lisa and her aunt both nodded.

Hollier closed the meeting and Lisa left to begin a new phase of her life with her unpleasant aunt, a life without the thrill of killing people.

Chapter 19 – Changes

Life at the aunt's house was not easy. Lisa moved in with her few possessions, acquired a small safe for her room and locked away the three Etruscan items. There were no questions about the safe. The Grimshaw family was massively wealthy and understood the concept of safe keeping and secrecy. She never opened the safe and so never put on the jewellery to experience the flood of killing lust or the sight of her face growing older in the mirror. The demon didn't appear.

There was little conversation at mealtimes and Lisa spent almost her entire time in the house in her own room, a radio and small television providing all the company she needed. It allowed Lisa to let her mind roam free and most of that time she mused on the possibilities of killing her aunt. But she realised that would be a fatal move, she'd be the obvious suspect from the start and would attract too much police attention.

At fifteen, she developed an interest in the boys at school. Her already mature looks attracted much attention, and she had no shortage of male company. But something wasn't quite as she expected.

She dated a few boys in the beginning and experienced some immature sexual adventures which she enjoyed, but she realised there was something different about them. Although she mildly enjoyed the physical exercise, several times during an encounter, she suddenly got the thrilling idea of how exciting it would be to kill the boy while he was preoccupied with his inexperienced gropes. When that idea erupted in her mind, her reaction to the episode became sharply enhanced in a torrent of erotic excitement, which always had a strong effect on the boy. She smiled to herself when she thought of how he would react if he knew what she was really thinking.

Pleasant as they were, the relationships never lasted more than two or three meetings. Each time, the boy seemed to lose interest and didn't ask for a further date. After a few months, the attentions of the boys withered away completely.

She made few friends among the girls. Initially, she seemed popular, and the other girls talked to her and exchanged giggly stories of their sexual encounters. But that too, died away. After the first year, she was entirely alone.

Lisa was more puzzled than distressed by the development. She had never felt the need for human companionship and her dating experience with Jake at the previous school had been more curiosity and the exercise of her sexual powers that had developed even at the age of twelve. But she had never felt any romantic urges then and still didn't in her teenage years. She had never comprehended the other girls at school when they had poured out their passions for particular boys.

One evening, she took to her room, locked the door and opened the safe.

The familiarity of the changes as she donned the items was a warm confirmation of who she was. The sight of the demon in the mirror and then her appearance in the room was a welcome return to an old routine. She felt no fear.

"Tell me something," she said. "Why do people move away from me after a while, especially the boys. Why do they walk away after we've dated for a couple of weeks?"

"It's what's inside you," said Vanth. "You may have a wonderful body, and you are generous with your access to it, and what teenage boy does not enjoy a good grope, however inexpert? But when the lust has been sated, they sense the killing drive inside you and it frightens them. The girls sense it too, and they are also frightened."

"What can I do?" Lisa felt the absolute correctness of Vanth's words. She knew that several times during the sexual encounters, the thought of killing the boy with her had erupted in her mind. It had given her additional pleasure and made the encounter more exciting for her.

"In time, this characteristic will prove invaluable for you when you return to your chosen path," said Vanth. "You must recover your independence and then you will be free to exploit your powers fully."

Lisa knew what she meant. A year later, as she turned sixteen, she contacted the lawyer and asserted her right to claim back her parents' house. There was no sadness, no fond farewells as she left the aunt's house. Everybody was relieved.

* * *

"Happy birthday, Lisa," said Benjamin Hollier. "And what a present for your eighteenth birthday, eh?"

"Thanks, Ben," said Lisa. "I opened a bank account when I was sixteen, as you advised me I could, so is everything ready?"

"It is. Your Uncle Simon signed all the papers to hand over the trust account to you yesterday, so you'll be a multi-millionaire already. I hope you've got professional advice on how to handle this vast sum?"

"I have, Ben. I have a licenced financial adviser and an established accounting firm."

"There's one more thing," said Hollier, consulting his file. "When your parents died and you moved out, I arranged for all their possessions, including clothing to be collected and stored away while the house was rented. But it was rented furnished, so everything is still there Now that the last tenants have left, everything else has been returned, including your parents' clothes. But the house is fully furnished, so it's fine to move in until you decide what to do."

"Oh, okay, thanks. I think I'll have the charity shops come and collect their clothes, if nothing else."

"I'll arrange that. Everything else is in a large cabin trunk, I'll ask the movers to leave that in your parents' room. Any ideas of what you will do now?"

"Go travelling. I'm going to buy a really good campervan and take it over the Channel and then just play it by ear. I got my passport when I was sixteen, I plan to cover Europe from Finland down to Italy. It's something I've dreamed of since I was a kid."

"Sounds marvellous. You will take care, won't you? Only stay in established camp sites, don't travel at night, don't pick up hitchhikers."

"I promise. Thanks for all the help."

Chapter 20 – Europe, and the Killing Continues

Lisa drove the campervan off the cross-channel ferry at Ostend and joined the line to go through the very casual immigration process. Swallowing the disappointment that her gleaming new passport didn't get stamped, she continued to the road and paused. Left or right? With a glow of excitement, she turned left, relishing the idea that she had total freedom in a way she had never experienced before.

Working hard to concentrate on driving on the right side of the road, she drove fairly slowly. She had driven through the night to catch the early morning crossing at Dover, and after two hours began to feel the sleepiness. Her timing was good, as she saw the signs for a camp site just ahead, and gratefully pulled in, checked in with the office and parked where was directed. She slept for five hours and woke to a beautiful early afternoon. After a shower and a change of clothes, she drove out and back on the road.

When she saw the hitchhiker, a jolt of excitement ran through her. She slowed and stopped by the young man with the Canadian flag sewn on his backpack.

"Hi," she said. "Where are you heading?"

She watched as he blinked in surprise at her looks, and she felt the warmth of something wonderful about to happen.

"Amsterdam," he said.

"Climb in." She watched him as he walked round the front of the vehicle and opened the left-hand door to enter. *A good body,* she thought, *about twenty, maybe. Perfect for what I want.* She moved the van on and soon they were following the highway again.

They chatted in amicable fashion, and she adopted the flirtatious manner she had perfected over the years. Judging by the way he kept looking sideways at her, she knew she had him hooked. When he looked out of the window at a particular scenic sight, she carefully undid a button on her blouse and shifted the garment to display the tops of her breasts. Twice, she put her hand on his thigh briefly. The technique worked perfectly.

After an hour of driving, as the heat in the cabin rose, she saw a pathway leading into the forest. She slowed and turned off, drove a few hundred metres into an area of close trees and bushes.

"We need to take a break," she said. "Come into the back with me."

Within moments, they were engaged in an enthusiastic coupling on the double bed. Clothes were shed and the young man was totally concentrated on working on Lisa's mostly naked body. The rush of excitement that flooded her was only partially from the sex. She reached down to the side of the bed where she had stowed a knife, one of several hidden away but easily accessible in the cabin, pulled it out, moved it under the man's stomach and thrust it hard into him. She watched his face, almost experiencing an orgasm as she saw the shock and the pain overwhelm him. She pulled out the blade and struck him again as blood poured all over her, then she pushed him off and got up, still watching him as he died. Never had she experienced such an erotic eruption as with this. Assured that he was dead, she opened the door and pushed the body out onto the grass.

Taking a rag from the basin, she wet it and wiped herself down as much as she could, singing softly as she did. She saw blood on the floor and continued cleaning up until she was sure that any casual inspection would find nothing. Dressing herself again, she drove back to the highway. Three hours later, she turned into another campsite. The shower block was a welcome sight, and she washed off the remaining traces of blood. Returning to the van, she saw a hosepipe in the general work area, moved the van to it and washed down the outside before opening the side door and rinsing down the floor with just a few small sprays of blood visible. She was sure that if anyone saw her, they would assume she was just washing down the vehicle.

She returned the van to its assigned parking spot and sat in the driver's seat, breathing deeply, reliving the experience of recent hours.

"That was the best ever," she said aloud. "Even if I don't find any Tarquinia, this trip has already been worth it."

The following day, she reached Amsterdam. For two days, she enjoyed being a tourist. She left the van in the campsite just outside the city and took a bus in to see the art museums, spending many hours in the famous Van Gogh Museum and Rijksmuseum, standing in awe in front of some of the most famous paintings in the world, forgetting what her real mission in life was.

But then the itch to kill started again. And it was almost a gift to her.

As she returned to the camp site early one evening, she saw a crowd of young people having a barbeque by the pool. She didn't approach them, trying to keep as least memorable as possible, but watched from behind the shower blocks.

Something assaulted her nostrils. Just for a few seconds, she couldn't identify what was happening, but then she did.

Tarquinia!

At first, she couldn't identify which of the eight or nine young people in the party had caused the reaction, but finally she did. Again, it was a young man, probably in his twenties, wearing jeans but no shirt. Briefly, she admired the man's body, but that was quickly overrun by the rage in her, the hatred and the killing lust. She stayed watching, trying to control the huge anger in her, and finally saw him walk away. Carefully, she followed and saw him enter a small tent. Whether it was big enough for two, she couldn't be sure. Noting the position, she returned to her campervan.

She couldn't sleep, the furious passion running through her body made that impossible. It was hard simply to wait for several hours, but at just after two, she slid the knife in its scabbard onto a belt and left the van, carrying a small towel. The night was dark, just a tiny sliver of a new moon providing a dim light through a thin cloud haze. Carefully, she navigated her way to the tent she had marked before and stood motionless for a few moments. She could hear only one person breathing deeply and her electric senses confirmed there was only the Tarquinian in the tent.

She sliced open the fastenings at the front and opened the flap. As she had known, there was just one person there. She slipped in and moved to the man's head. The smell of beer was strong, and she realised the man was quite drunk. He was lying on his side, but his neck was easily visible.

In one smooth motion, she sliced the sharp blade across his throat and held the towel across the cut to stem the blood. For a moment, he struggled, but her grip on his neck held him down and it was only a few seconds before he collapsed and went still.

Leaving the towel where it was, she slid out and walked back to the van, making no noise. Opening the door and closing it carefully behind her, she washed the blade in the sink, wiped it down from tip to handle and replaced it in its hiding place.

She slept well until dawn.

She woke to the sounds of screams. Smiling to herself, she knew what the sound indicated. Dressing rapidly in shorts and tee-shirt, she went outside and to the source of the noise. A crowd had gathered, mostly of the young people from last night, but as she stood, the manager from the camp office ran up. There was an agitated conversation between him and the girl who had discovered the body and was having trouble in speaking while distraught with tears. Within minutes, the police arrived in two cars. While one man crawled into the tent and flashes from a camera were visible, two others rapidly erected a barrier of a single ribbon round the tent.

A uniformed policewoman addressed the crowd through a loudspeaker. Lisa could not understand her as she seemed to speak in three different languages, though she recognised French and German if not the first. But then the words were in English.

"Go back to your tents or campervans," said the young woman. "Stay there until we come and talk to you. You may not leave the site until then."

Impressed by the multiple languages, Lisa did as ordered. The day had warmed up a little, so she moved a folding chair outside and took a book to read, which allowed her to keep one eye on the activities by the murder scene.

Eventually, a female officer walked up to her. It was the woman who had addressed the crowd earlier.

"When did you arrive at the site, Miss Kendricks?" she asked.

"Yesterday, about three."

The officer consulted her notepad and nodded. "That agrees with the check-in time. Did you know anyone in the group having their barbeque when you arrived?"

"No, I didn't." Lisa was impressed by the absence of any accent in the officer's voice.

"And when did you arrive in Europe?"

"Two days ago, at Ostend by ferry from Dover."

The officer consulted her telephone, entered a few digits and waited briefly.

"That checks," she said. "Where will you be heading after this stay?"

"Amsterdam. After that, no fixed route."

Thank you, Miss Kendricks. Enjoy your time in Europe."

Clearly, she saw nothing suspicious in Lisa. Lisa imagined that one of the dead man's party would be the most likely candidate, or just a casual intruder during the night who had already left.

Lisa made herself breakfast and ate in the van, the radio picking up an English station with the news of the day. There was nothing that interested her and Lisa decided to move on later, feeling well satisfied with the events of her trip so far.

Chapter 21 – More of Europe

For two more months, Lisa continued to drive around Europe. Sometimes she killed a person, two of them were revealed as Tarquinia, as even the tiniest trace in the individual's DNA could be detected by her hypersensitive nose. After Amsterdam, she continued on through northern Europe to Helsinki. The easiest killings were like the very first, hitchhikers who could be seduced into a woodland setting and easily killed. There were three of those, but none of them was Tarquinia, just objects to satisfy her well-developed lust for killing. Nobody in Helsinki set off her Tarquinia alarm.

The next Tarquinian she encountered was in Hannover in Germany. White eating lunch in a diner, she sensed the arrival of an elderly woman with a small child. They sat a few tables from her and talked as grandparents talked to their much-loved grandchildren. Suppressing the torrent of rage and hatred that threatened to drown her, Lisa waited until the two left and followed them. She had parked her van in the public area for the diner and was relieved to see that the woman was parked just three places away.

When the woman drove off, Lisa carefully followed her, watched as she dropped off the child at an apartment block and continued to a small house further out of town. Lisa drove a kilometre away and waited till nightfall. Soon after ten, she walked back to the house and rang the doorbell. The woman seemed to have no suspicions about a late caller and answered the door. Lisa shoved it open, walked in and stabbed the woman in the heart. As the body dropped, Lisa walked out, closed the door and went back to her van. The suburb had been quiet, probably a popular area for retirees and Lisa was sure nobody had seen her. The anger was replaced with a huge sense of fulfilment.

Another male hitchhiker fell to Lisa's well-established technique in Switzerland and then she arrived in Italy, crossing from France into the territory that had once been the Etruscan Empire. She felt no emotional sensation on returning to the places she had visited with her father several years earlier, just disappointment that she had met no more Tarquinian descendants. Even within the homes and tombs of the Vulci and Tarquinian families, she felt nothing.

The same emptiness was encountered all through Italy, down to Rome and Naples, then back up to Milan and Pisa, not a sniff of the hated Tarquinia anywhere. Nor did the situation improve for her all the way up through France, back on the ferry and home again.

Lisa opened her safe and took out the three Etruscan ornaments. Sitting comfortably in her lounge room, rather than in her bedroom, she donned the items. She no longer needed the mirror, and Vanth, the Angel of Death appeared almost immediately.

"Have the Tarquinia vanished from Europe?" Lisa asked in anger. "This was almost a wasted trip. I found only three."

"But you killed several other people," replied Vanth. She appeared to sit comfortably in an armchair and she wore a small smile. She was back in conventional, modern clothing, this time a business suit in black with a white blouse. She could be any senior executive in a bank or accounting firm.

"They were like a snack between meals," said Lisa. "Only killing a Tarquinia is satisfying. Where are they all?"

"They're still lots of them around, just as there are many Vulci descendants. You didn't get to meet them."

"So what's the point of wearing this responsibility if I can't apply it?" Lisa's anger was growing. She sensed the rage inside her becoming almost out of control and fought to suppress it.

"Do you think you could kill every Tarquinian descendant in the world?"

Hearing the sarcasm in the voice almost drove Lisa over the edge. She knew the demon was laughing at her and she struggled to control herself.

"No, I don't. But I'm only eighteen. I was assuming I could keep killing those scum until I get old."

"You might find a few more," said Vanth. "But that might require you to travel the world, hoping to find the very few victims for your hatred among the hundreds of millions of people. A needle in a haystack is a feast of needles by comparison."

"Why didn't you warn me of this?"

"Why should I? I'm merely the facilitator for your orgy. Of course, you realise you are going to Hell when you die?"

Lisa laughed. "Hell? There is no Hell, no Heaven, those are just inventions of the Churches to scare the peasants and keep them in line."

"Oh, there is a Hell alright. But it's an Etruscan Hell, it has always been a part of our existence. It's something we gave the other churches and various religions, they copied the idea and found it useful, but they don't have one."

"So how come you have a Hell?" Lisa was still contemptuous. "What's so different about Etruscans?"

"Lisa, you disappoint me." Vanth appeared to grow a little larger and Lisa felt a sudden quiver of fear. *What was happening?*

"Your father was considered one of the greatest experts in the world on my people," continued the frightening shape in the other chair. "And yet he was never able to be certain where the Etruscans originated. He spouted theories based on DNA, just as the other so-called experts did, but they never came close to the truth."

Despite her increasing fear, Lisa sensed a growing interest. Was she about to learn a massive truth that had baffled the world for centuries?

"Lisa, the Etruscans are not any branch of humans that science has identified. They are not related to Cro-Magnon man, nor from the Neanderthals, they are unique. They didn't migrate from their original places in a remote part of Asia and were never identified. Eventually, they migrated to the part of Northern Italy that has become known as their base, but they are unlike any species of humans."

"And they have their own real Hell?" For a moment, Lisa's fear was submerged beneath the interest. "And only Etruscans go there?"

Vanth nodded. "As will you. And it will be my duty to escort you there"

"Me? But why?" Lisa's terror returned.

"Do you think you could kill so many of your own people and escape punishment?" The demon was openly mocking her.

"But I was following the curse," she cried. "I had no choice."

"You'd be amazed at how many mass killers have made that call. From killers throughout history, claiming they were just following orders has been the standard excuse. But you are a little more unfortunate. You really did have no choice. When the Vulci and the Tarquinia exchanged their curses on each other, I added a small price without their knowledge. I placed an added price on whoever wore the cursed ornaments, that they would go to Hell when their time was over."

Lisa hid her face in her hands. "Is there anything I can do?"

"Nothing. You must continue killing Tarquinia when you encounter them, because not to do so will kill you in great pain. Only the act of killing keeps you alive now. The more you kill, whether Tarquinia or not, the longer you will live."

Lisa regained control of herself and her terror. "Then I will continue to kill. And if I meet a Tarquinian, that will be a wonderful feast among the snacks."

"Agreed," said Vanth. "But first, let me show you what faces you some time in the future."

With no sense of movement, Lisa found herself in a dark, gloomy corridor. It was narrow, claustrophobic and oppressive. Vanth was standing behind her.

"In here," she said and the wall to one side became transparent. In the space now revealed, a single man stood silently. He was dressed in medieval clothing, a fur jacket, heavy trousers and a cloth hat. From nowhere, a shape appeared out of the gloom, leaped on the man and stabbed him with a heavy dagger. The man screamed in pain, sank to his knees, head bowed. The attacker stabbed him again in the back of the neck and the man collapsed, bleeding heavily, though still alive. The attacker was revealed as a young woman, her clothing drenched in blood, and she stood over the dying man, laughing.

"That is the scene when the Tarquinia family summoned a demon to defend themselves against the

Vulci curse," said Vanth. "The man is Vel Tarquinia and the girl is the serving girl he killed as the price of summoning me. This is his price. He will experience being killed that way again and again, always feeling the agony of his death for a thousand years. This is her revenge."

As Lisa stood there, the scene flickered back to when she had first seen it. Vel Tarquinia stood motionless, the girl appeared and stabbed him twice as he fell, lying in blood as his body twitched and finally went still.

"A thousand years?" Lisa was horrified.

"That is the standard sentence," said Vanth.

"And what happens then?"

"He will disappear. I believe he will then join the rest of the human race in standard death."

"You don't know what happens?"

"I don't," said the demon.

"And is that what will happen to me?" Lisa's voice shook a little.

"That is your future. You will experience death at the hands of every one of your victims, in the same manner as you killed them, time and time again for a thousand years."

And Lisa was back in her lounge room. There was no sign of the Angel of Death.

Chapter 22 – A Year in Retreat

For a year, Lisa retreated from the world. She slept heavily and although she woke knowing that she had experienced dreadful nightmares, there was no memory of them. The shock of the last meeting she'd had with the demon left her almost lifeless. Waking late, well after eleven, she rarely dressed beyond pyjamas and a dressing gown, her hair was a mess, and her bodily hygiene suffered. She never went out, ordered food delivered from the local supermarket, but occasionally forgot to eat all day. She lost a quarter of her body weight.

Slowly, she began to return to the world. Waking up one day, she was repulsed by the mess she had become. The smell was rank and when she looked in the mirror, she almost screamed. That day, she showered, dressed, even though casually in jeans and a shirt, and walked outside into the back garden. The mess and decay in what had been her mother's great joy was almost as severe a shock as the image of herself.

It took half a day to work up some energy, but by later afternoon, she had found the telephone number of the gardener who had managed the lawn and flower beds years before and asked him to come and start the repair work. That evening, she switched on the television for the first time in twelve months and began catching up on the world's news. That gave her no cause for cheerfulness, but she persisted, knowing she had to be part of events.

She had lost all memory of the talk with the demon and her visit to Etruscan hell. She knew of her deep depression but had no idea of the cause. Two days later, she called up a beauty parlour in town and made an appointment.

"Oh my," said the pretty teenager when Lisa walked in. "You look like you really need some help."

"I've been ill for a while, caught something while working in a village in Africa," said Lisa.

"Sit down," said the girl firmly, and the process began.

An hour later, Lisa left, another appointment booked in two days' time, beginning to feel like her old self. Another intensive session of repair brought her almost to a sense of normality. That evening, she cooked a proper meal and ate with enjoyment.

She still had no memory of the conversation with the demon. But some other parts of her memory returned, and with them some needs.

On the Saturday night, she carefully dressed herself in a gown she found in her wardrobe. With her much reduced size, the gown was very loose on her, but it seemed to add to the erotic nature of her image, revealing more than usual area of skin. She had no memory of ever having bought it, but when she was dressed, in high heels and her hair freshly brushed, the image in the mirror pleased her. She decided on a cab to the club she remembered from earlier years and when she entered to hear the strong beat of the music, she knew she had done the right thing.

For an hour, she danced almost full time, having no shortage of young men advance on her. After several had danced with her, she had selected the one she considered most suitable. As she passed him, while in the arms of one very persistent man, she gave him her best invitation look. As expected, the next dance was with him and she deliberately snuggled up, pressed her body against his and put her hand on his neck. She felt his response and matched it. Half an hour later, they were in her bedroom, engaged in highly active sex. After a short sleep, they returned to awareness.

"You're not staying for breakfast," she said.

"Why not? Surely we've deserved it, there's more action to come." The man seemed astonished.

"No. I don't like sleeping with somebody after we've had sex."

"Why the hell not? Wasn't I good enough?"

"You were fine, great even. But I don't want you to stay. Please go now."

"Jesus, what a bitch." The man got up, found his clothes and left, anger showing in the rigid stance as he walked out of the bedroom.

Lisa fell asleep again, well satisfied with the night.

The following week, she repeated the exercise with much the same results. With her mental state returning to normal and her physical health responding to her improved diet, Lisa began to realise that there were great gaps in her memory. One morning, after a long breakfast, she saw the small safe she had acquired while living with her aunt.

"What the hell have I got in there?" she said aloud. She looked at the lock and saw it required a digital code to undo. "Did I set a code when I got the thing?" she muttered. "Where the hell would I find it?"

She decided that logical place to start looking was in her possessions in her room. There was not a lot of material to seek through, but when she saw her long-discarded diary in the bookshelf, she felt that this could be the answer. She began leafing through the book, page by page. There were no entries for the previous year, but in among the personal details was a six-figure number in a space of its own. Her heart jumped, feeling sure that this was what she was seeking.

She carried the book down to the safe and tried setting those numbers in sequence. But the door wouldn't open.

"Damn," she said aloud. "Now what? Think, Lisa, what would you do if you were setting the code and storing the number where somebody might find it, but couldn't use it? How about just reversing the digits?"

Once more, she entered the six digits but got no success. She felt her temper rising. After several efforts using different sequences, she was about to give up, swearing hard at the safe. Finally, she tried entering the second three digits followed by the first three.

The door clicked. Lisa let out a whoop of triumph and opened the door.

Lying on a velvet cloth, she saw the gold necklace, the gold ring and the copper bracelet. She was overwhelmed by the emotions flooding through her. Vividly, she remembered each of the killings she had performed, the violence of the hatred when she identified a Tarquinian descendant and the wonderful satisfaction she felt when she killed one.

For a long time, she sat in front of the safe, staring at the ornaments, but she didn't take them from the safe. She had no idea why, but somehow, she felt reluctant. She closed the safe door and locked it again. She remained puzzled by her behaviour.

For another month, she followed the new pattern of life she had found when she woke from the year-long dark shadow. And then everything changed.

* * *

Lisa woke up feeling sick. She ran to the bathroom and puked violently into the toilet bowl. Feeling most unwell, she returned to her bed but was unable to fall sleep again. She called a local medical centre but was unable to get an immediate appointment. The receptionist at the clinic suggested she should go to the emergency ward at the local hospital. Lisa got the car out of the garage and drove to the hospital in the middle of the town. She had only about half an hour to wait.

"Miss Kendricks, there's no doubt. You're pregnant, about eight weeks along." The young woman doctor pulled off her rubber gloves and smiled. "Everything looks quite normal, you have a very healthy foetus."

Lisa was badly shaken. The thought of falling pregnant after the several sexual encounters she'd had in the last few weeks had never occurred to her.

"I realise this may not be the most welcome news, being single, so what do you think you want to do?" continued the doctor.

To her own surprise, Lisa knew the answer quite clearly.

"I'll keep it," she said. "This is wonderful."

"Excellent," said the doctor.

"You will abort it," said a voice behind her as Lisa watched television that evening.

Lisa jerked upright and turned round. For the first time in over a year, the demon was standing in the room.

"No, I won't," retorted Lisa. "This is my chance to live something like a normal life after my last ten years. Whatever faces me when I die, at least I can make up for some of the deaths I've caused by raising a normal child."

"That is not your destiny. You will abort the foetus. It is male, and the mission cannot succeed with a boy.

The curse can only continue with a female not yet into maidenhood, just as you were when it fell onto you."

Lisa shivered. There was powerful menace in Vanth's voice.

"And what if I don't?"

"Then I will abort it. And I promise, the pain you will go through will be far worse than if you did it under proper medical procedures."

Lisa had no doubts she was telling her the truth. For the first time, she understood the evil that the shape before her represented.

"And when that is done, you will again put on the three Vulci ornaments and return to your destiny."

"And what is that?"

"You know very well. You are a Vulci, and your destiny is to kill Tarquinia. You have no other path in life."

Lisa burst into tears, but later, she made the appointment to see the hospital and arrange the termination of her pregnancy.

Chapter 23 – Normal Service Resumed

Lisa sat before the mirror of her dressing table and slowly donned each of the ornaments in turn. As she put on the necklace, old, familiar senses flooded her body. She felt the maturity, the commitment to a path of killing, the deep hatred of the Tarquinia family. She added the ring and the whole tide of emotions got stronger.

Deep inside her, she detected just a tiny voice pleading to be allowed to return, but she could no longer remember the child, Lisa, who had played with dolls, talked about a future as a wife and a mother, who had friends of her age who valued her company and didn't shrink away at the sight of her. Then she slid the copper bracelet onto her wrist and the tiny voice vanished. Lisa had no memory of who and what she had been before the Vulci family took over her soul.

She studied her image in the mirror. It was no longer the face of a youthful woman. Now she was older, mid-fifties, with lines around her eyes and in her upper lip. There was no warmth in that face, nothing but cold distaste for everyone around.

"Is this what I become?" she asked herself, not liking the answer. A rising emotion became stronger as she looked. She knew what it was.

She had to kill again.

For an hour, she sat and looked at her changed image, thinking about how she would achieve the goal. She realised that apart from killing Tarquinia, the most pleasurable and fulfilling murders had been those where she killed a young man while engaged in active sex play, and she decided this would be the means of slaking the thirst. But she realised that after the last session with the man from the dance club, she might be recognised and perhaps referred to any police investigation. She started planning.

It took a day to dye her hair blonde and match the colour in her eyebrows. She searched through her wardrobe and found a plaid skirt she had worn in her teenage years, short enough to attract attention, but long enough to hide the knife in its scabbard she would hang at her waist. The white blouse was cut deep enough to pull every male eye. She found a pair of high-heeled shoes she had worn in that same time. They hurt the feet terribly, but they added height and together with the other changes, would not easily link her to the more conventional image she had shown the last time she went to a club.

The effect she had was shown the minute she walked into the club she had found in the Internet, an hour's drive from her house. She was conscious of numerous male faces turned in her direction and she took a seat by the wall, knowing she would not sit there for long.

As before, she was engaged from the very first, several men lining up to ask her to dance, obviously competing with each other and providing her with amusement as she saw the tempers rising with several of them as they failed to get her onto the dance floor. Finally, she selected her victim, cuddled up to him and pressed her body to his.

"Can we get out of here?" she murmured into the man's ear.

"You bet," he replied. "My car's just outside."

She let him lead them out, submissively holding his hand and followed him out of the building, just a few yards to where he had a small saloon car parked. When he had seated her and closed the door, taken the driver's seat and started the engine, she put the next part of the plan into effect.

"I know the perfect place," she said softly. "It's in the woods, just off the road and very sheltered."

She directed him to a spot she had found in recent days. He parked the car and let her out, almost unable to stop clutching at her body. She laughed and led him to the selected spot. In the soft grass, she lay back and let him get to work. As he penetrated her and began heaving, she slipped her hand to her waist, pulled out the knife, pushing it hard into his body. He screamed and rolled off her, clutching at the wound. She pulled out the knife and repeated the blow, the knife digging deep until it struck bone. Lisa stood up, almost feeling an orgasm as she watched the man die as the light faded from his eyes, leaving an expression of deep horror in his face.

Lisa extracted light gloves and a plastic raincoat from her large handbag, the last part of the planning, donned them and bent down to extract the man's keys from his pocket.

"Have a nice night," she said and took the car. Leaving it in the carpark of a pub, she walked the final kilometre home, her feet hurting badly. But when she got back to her house, she let herself in, gratefully took off the shoes and bundled the plastic raincoat and her other clothes into the incinerator. It took two days for the blonde colour to be washed away from her hair and eyebrows, and she didn't leave the house in that time.

She was well satisfied with the killing and enjoyed watching local television news items about the body found in the woods, the mysterious blonde woman who had been seen leaving the dance hall with the victim, knowing she had left no clues to incriminate her.

It was satisfying, but nothing like the sheer wonder of killing a Tarquinian.

Chapter 24 – The Hounds Awaken

Detective Sergeant Mary Stanton enjoyed her job, though sometimes, the ugliness and cruelty she encountered in people distressed her. One part of her job that gave her some respite from the encounters with the worst characteristics of humans was to research the updates she received from other police regions of Britain and Europe. Over the years, she had acquired a reputation of which she was very proud, that of sniffing out hints, clues and connections between crimes that had been missed by law enforcement operations in those areas.

On this day, she was concentrating hard on files from the last two years that she had downloaded to her computer. She ran lists sorted by location of murders, then by mode of killing, by victim type and finally by suspect type.

As she finished the last of her fourth mug of coffee that morning and sat back to think about what she had found, something nagged at her. There was a trend with several of these events, occurring in both Europe and in England. She accessed another data base from a government department that held details of travellers between England and the continent and finally, records of cross-channel ferries.

The mental eruption in her head was almost like a brilliant light switching on. For a moment, she was out of breath as if she had sprinted across town, but she settled down and extracted the records that had triggered the light and printed out two sheets that told a remarkable story.

Then she picked up her phone and called Detective Chief Inspector Adrian Cooper who had been her superior for some years. She also called Detective Inspector James Brigham. Some years before, all three had been involved in a curious case of serial killings that had never been solved.

The appointment was set for that afternoon.

"Okay, spill it," said Cooper. Over the years he had developed great respect and admiration for Mary's investigative and research skills, and he had no doubt that this meeting would reveal something valuable.

"Over the last two years, there have been six almost identical murders in Europe and here in England. All of them were killings of young men, stabbed with a sharp knife in the torso and the bodies left in woodland, not far from a major road. The first five took place between two years and eighteen months ago. The one here was the latest, just a few weeks ago."

"And where here?" asked Detective Inspector James Brigham.

"I'm glad you asked that," said Mary with a smug smile. "Because we all know about it. It was right here in the Leyland Woods. Andrew Foster, aged twenty-eight was found by a dog walker, stabbed twice and left in a clearing. His clothing indicated he'd been engaged in sexual activity when he was killed."

"Right," said Brigham. "Carry on, Sergeant."

Mary hid her smile. She was used to bearing the load of providing evidence when with her two superior officers.

"There were eyewitnesses who said he had left the club with a blonde woman in standard man-catching gear," she continued. "Nobody recognised her, and nobody has ever come forward with an identification."

"His car was found in the parking lot of the Baron Snellgrove pub," added Cooper. "SOCO tore the car to pieces, but they couldn't find a single clue to the last driver who put it there. There was a tiny trace of plastic on the seat, suggesting the driver had worn a plastic raincoat of some sort and there were indications that she had worn stiletto high-heeled shoes, as a couple of sharp dents in the floor carpet were found."

"So this blonde, whoever she is, had planned this carefully," said Mary.

"It would seem so," agreed Cooper. "Okay, Mary, now tell us what's got your gander up."

"Let me review a bit first," replied Mary. She could see that the two men were listening carefully, obviously interested in what she was telling them. "The five men killed in Europe were all hitchhikers, according to police reports. Now this is where it gets interesting. I compared the dates of the killings with dates of vehicle transits from England and around Europe. Like here, there are numerous road cameras that record the passage of vehicles and their speeds. And this is what I found."

She smiled at her senior colleagues. They knew her well enough to be certain she was imparting critical information, and she had their full attention.

"Two days before the first hitchhiker was found near the E40 road from Ostend to Amsterdam, a white campervan crossed that morning from Dover to Ostend and was later filmed on the road past Ostend on the way to Amsterdam."

"And why is that campervan the vehicle that got your attention?" Cooper was sitting upright. "Surely there were plenty of other holidaymakers doing the same route?"

"Because it's owned by somebody we know from our past investigations, Lisa Kendricks." Mary sensed the shock this caused in her colleagues.

"Jake Cahill," said Brigham. "Found garrotted twelve years ago in the Leyland Woods, believed to be the boyfriend of Lisa Kendricks, but nothing could be established to show her involvement."

"And Peter Franklin and Dylan Marlow," added Cooper. "Assumed to be a murder suicide, both deaths by stabbing after killing Jake Cahill, found in those same woods. Also known to be associates of Lisa Kendricks. Mary, you raised these connections when we met after the killing of Jake Cahill. And then you added the killings of her parents. That meant Lisa was connected in some way with more than half the murders up till then."

"Holy shit," said Brigham.

"Exactly," said Mary. "When James and I interviewed Lisa, I commented then that if she was fourteen years old, I was the Queen of Sheba," said Mary.

"I remember that," said Brigham. "I think I said something like she was fourteen going on thirty."

"Far too composed for anyone of that age," added Mary.

"But throwing some doubts on Lisa Kendricks is interesting," said Cooper, sitting back in his seat. "And we sure as hell will be investigating her again, but she's not a blonde, or wasn't the last time I saw her all those years ago. What else has your digging revealed?"

"There is stuff called hair dye," said Mary with a smile and returned to her papers. "And now it gets better and better. I was able to get transit camera records on the routes near where the other four killings of hitchhikers occurred. The day the second one was discovered, on the A3 highway forty kilometres from Cologne, the same white van was recorded the previous day heading to Cologne."

"Oh Jesus," muttered Cooper. "What sort of monster have we got here?"

"Stay with me, sir," said Mary. "The third body was found sixty kilometres from Luxemburg on the road from Cologne, a week later. Lisa Kendricks stayed in a camp site outside Cologne for four days and then was recorded on the road to Luxemburg two days before the body was found."

"I'm not sure I can take any more of this," muttered Cooper. "But you have more?"

"Two more," said Mary. "But let me summarise. "Lisa's campervan was recorded on the road near Lake Como, heading to Milan six days later. Two days after that, a body was found near the road in woodland. Finally, I can link her to a body found south of Milan and the van seen on the road near that spot."

"And when did Lisa return to England?" asked Cooper.

"Eighteen months ago."

"And this latest killing two weeks ago is the only one of its kind since then?"

"Yes, it is, sir."

"Then you two need to go and talk to her again."

"Yes, sir," said Brigham. "Great work, Mary." Both he and Mary left the Chief Inspector's office.

* * *

"Miss Lisa Kendricks?" I'm Detective.."

"Sergeant Brigham. Yes, I remember you. And this woman is Detective Constable Mary Stanton, correct?"

"That's very impressive, Miss Kendricks," said Brigham. "It was over five years ago."

"That you interrogated me about the murder of Jake Cahill, yes, I remember."

Brigham showed his warrant card. "Let me update you. I am Detective Inspector Brigham, and my colleague is Detective Sergeant Stanton. May we come in?"

Showing no reaction, Lisa stood aside and led the two detectives to a lounge room. She sat in an armchair and waited for the others to seat themselves, Brigham in the opposite armchair and Mary on the settee. The room looked a little seedy, the furniture was old, and the wallpaper had faded a little. Mary estimated it was exactly as it had been five years ago when they had visited for the second time after Lisa's parents had been killed.

Now why would this be? she thought. *She's a multi-millionaire, why would she leave the house to decline like this? Where have her interests been directed?*

"So how can I help you?" asked Lisa.

"We are investigating the murder of Andrew Foster who was found dead in Leyland Woods ten days ago," said Brigham.

"So who is Andrew Foster?" asked Lisa with a puzzled expression. "And what do I have to do with his murder?"

"We didn't say he was murdered," said Mary.

Lisa looked annoyed. "You said he was found dead in the woods and you're interrogating me. What do you think I might conclude? That he died of a drug overdose in the woods, or something?"

Mary shrugged her shoulders. "That would actually be a logical possibility." *The bitch is playing with me. This is not a normal woman, just like I thought the last time I saw her.*

"Sure," said Lisa. "But I heard on the news that this bloke had been found stabbed in the woods a few days ago. So your "gotcha" moment didn't work, Detective Sergeant. Congratulations on the promotion, by the way, both of you."

"Thank you," said Mary. *I'll really enjoy arresting this bitch, if we get to it. I'm going to work hard to achieve that. She knows something and she's not telling.*

"What is interesting to us," broke in Brigham, "is that we talked to you the last time, because your boyfriend, Jake Cahill had been found dead in that same spot."

"Garrotted, but not stabbed," said Lisa. "And that was reported on the news at the time, so not another "gotcha," detectives. And you concluded then that he had been killed by two kids from the same school."

"The same school as you, also," said Brigham. "And they're both dead, too, violent deaths in the same area as Jake Cahill had been killed. You do seem to be connected to a lot of suspicious deaths, Lisa."

"It's a small town," said Lisa. "Almost all the kids around here go to that school, so no coincidence there."

Brigham exchanged a quick look with Mary Stanton that said, *"She's playing with us."* Mary agreed fully.

"Let's move on to something else," said Brigham. "You came back last year from an extensive trip around Europe in your campervan, correct?"

Uh-oh, thought Mary. *She did not expect that. She went very still for a few seconds. This is getting interesting.*

"Yes, I did," Lisa replied after a few seconds' pause. "A life-long dream, and now I have the money, I decided to do it."

"A wonderful idea," said Brigham. "Looks like you crossed to Ostend, drove to Amsterdam, then to Cologne, Luxemburg, Geneva and Milan before heading back home through France to Calais where you boarded the ferry back to Dover."

Lisa stared at him. "You've been tracking me? Why the hell have you been tracking me? What's all this about?"

Her voice got progressively louder until the final words were a shriek.

This has really kicked her hard, thought Mary. *I'll lay heavy odds that she's involved one way or the other with the killings.*

Brigham was unmoved.

"Let me tell you what else we know," he said. "Five times during that trip, a dead man was found near the road that you had travelled just a day or two before.

Every one of those men was in his twenties, a hitchhiker, all died by stab wounds from what appears to be the same weapon. Do you have anything to say about that, Lisa?"

Lisa glared at him. She looked shaken by his words but not frightened.

"No," she said. "That's just coincidence. There are thousands of people driving those routes at this time of the year. I bet you could link dozens of them to those dead bodies. It's time for you two to fuck off out of my house."

Brigham stood up.

"Of course," he said. "But we may need to talk to you again."

"Just fuck off," said Lisa.

"Before I go, could I just use your bathroom?" asked Mary.

"No, you bloody can't," snapped Lisa. "That's where you planned to dump a few packets of some illegal drugs and then arrest me, isn't it?"

"Please, Lisa," said Mary as subserviently as possible. "I really need to go. I promise you, I'm not carrying any drugs on me."

"Oh hell, go and have your pee," retorted Lisa. "Then both of you, get the hell out of my house."

Mary walked quickly up the stairs, found the bathroom and looked around. She opened the cabinet and immediately saw what she suspected, a bottle of blonde hair dye. She couldn't take it, she was in the house without a warrant, at the invitation of the resident, but the sight confirmed her view. Waiting a few moments, she flushed the toilet and returned downstairs.

"Thank you," she said.

"Fuck off," said Lisa.

Brigham and Mary walked out and returned to the car.

"She's guilty as sin," said Mary. "The blonde hair dye is in her cabinet."

"Time to get a warrant," said Brigham. "Good work, Mary."

* * *

"This isn't supposed to be happening," said Lisa. She spoke loudly, reflecting her anger and some fear. "Those bastards are on to me. You were supposed to keep them away from me."

"And I will," replied Vanth. "Stop panicking." Her image appeared to be sitting comfortably in an armchair in Lisa's lounge. Nobody else could have seen her, but Lisa didn't realise that. She looked like any middle-aged woman dressed in modern casual clothing, as if about to head off for a round of golf.

"How can I stop panicking? They obviously know I killed those people in Europe, even if they haven't worked out the Tarquinians I killed. But they've got real evidence about the hitchhikers."

"Have you no faith in me? They had enough circumstantial evidence to get you for the deaths of your friends at school, but I turned their minds away. I'll do the same now."

With a soundless flick, she vanished. Lisa tried to calm herself with little success.

Chapter 25 – the Hounds Get the Scent

"What the hell?" said Lisa. "You two again? I told you before, fuck off and leave me alone." She tried to shut the door in the faces of Brigham and Stanton, but the Inspector put a size eleven boot in the way and flourished his warrant card.

"Lisa Kendrick," he said. "I am arresting you on suspicion of the murder of Andrew Foster and five additional murders of people to be named later, in The Netherlands, Germany and Italy. You do not have to say anything, but anything you say will be taken down and may be used in evidence against you. Do you understand?"

Lisa stood motionless, deeply shocked and frightened. *Surely this wasn't supposed to happen?* She stayed silent.

"We have a warrant to search these premises," continued Brigham. "Please move aside and let us enter."

Almost frozen into immobility, Lisa obeyed, and the two detectives walked past her into the house.

With a small gesture, Brigham signalled to Mary Stanton to take the upstairs. She nodded and moved to the staircase, heading straight to the bathroom. There she opened the cabinet and stopped. The bottle of blonde hair dye she had seen before was not there.

"Oh shit," she muttered aloud. "That's awkward. That's the only real evidence we would have, the rest is all circumstantial." She spent several minutes looking further in every corner of the bathroom, including the small garbage bin, but found nothing. Leaving the room, she located Lisa's bedroom and spent several minutes looking in every possible spot, still unsuccessfully. The provocatively-dressed blonde seen leaving with Andrew Foster from the dance club had clearly described as had the short skirt and low-cut white blouse she was wearing, but these were nowhere to be found, nor was any sort of plastic coat that might have kept bloodstains from the seat of Foster's car.

Feeling some anxiety, Mary returned downstairs and gave Brigham a tiny shake of her head. Showing no reaction, he began to lead Lisa to the front door.

"Normal practice is to put you in handcuffs," he said, holding firmly onto her left arm. "If you promise to behave, I won't do that, but one excuse, and I will. Is that understood, Lisa?"

She said nothing and Mary joined them, holding lightly to Lisa's right arm. They left the house and reached the car parked by the front gate. They guided Lisa into the back seat where was joined by Mary, and then Brigham drove to the police station.

Lisa said nothing, as if in deep shock as she was processed by the desk sergeant and then escorted to a cell. She sat on the bench and stared at the opposite wall as the door was closed behind her. She had not said a word since Brigham had arrested her.

"Shit," said Mary as the two detectives walked back to Brigham's office. "We'll have a problem here. She must have thrown out the hair dye after we were there last. And there was no sign of the clothes the blonde was reported to be wearing, nor any plastic covering. Any signs of a possible weapon?"

Brigham shook his head. "I doubt the Crown Prosecutor will want to proceed with only circumstantial evidence."

"A hell of a lot of circumstantial evidence," protested Mary. "It could work."

"Maybe," said Brigham.

Two hours later, they learnt more.

"I am Gerald Rex," said the tall, middle-aged man in a dark, well-cut suit. "I am the lawyer for Lisa Kendricks. You have her in custody on the most trumped-up charges I have ever encountered, and I demand her release at once."

"You have a card?" asked Brigham.

"Of course." The lawyer produced a business card and Mary studied it. It confirmed the man's name and profession, with an address in London. He appeared to be a sole practitioner, no partners were cited. She nodded at Brigham.

"Make your case," said the Inspector.

"Easy," said the visitor. "You have no evidence tying my client to any suspicious deaths. She does not resemble in any way the woman seen leaving with the deceased from the dance club. You may have noticed, my client is brunette, not blonde, you have seen no clothes in her house like those reported the blonde was wearing, so nobody has ever seen her in the company of the deceased."

He smiled a cold smile at the detectives. The face he showed made Mary shiver a little. There was something deeply disturbing about this man.

"And as for those deaths in Europe, what evidence do you have?" the visitor continued. "The fact that Ms Kendricks' campervan passed the general region a few days before the bodies were found, so what? Thousands of vehicles passed those spots every day and the route is hardly uncommon. Really, detectives, do you seriously think the Crown Prosecutor will show any interest in this case? You're making fools of yourselves."

Mary felt confidence draining away. She saw that Brigham was looking confused and angry. Neither of them spoke.

"Thank you," said the lawyer. "Please tell the desk sergeant to release my client and I will take her home."

Not saying anything, Brigham picked up the phone. He had to clear his throat and finally spoke. "Garry, release Lisa Kendrick. Yes, I know what I'm saying, release her now." He replaced the phone.

The lawyer stood up and left without another word.

There was silence in Brigham's office for a few moments before the Inspector picked up the lawyer's card.

"He's London-based?" he said. "How did he know

about Lisa's arrest? She didn't communicate with anyone after we arrested her. And how did he get here so quickly? It's at least three hours from London."

"There's something terribly wrong," said Mary. Confusion was rising in her mind like rising flood waters, and she was having difficulty remembering the image of the lawyer or what had been said.

Brigham turned to his computer and entered a few keystrokes. He waited a few moments.

"There's no such lawyer in the data base," he said. "And I know we've never had any dealings with him."

"But.." began Mary, then confusion overwhelmed her. She could not recall the lawyer's face, nor even the arrest of Lisa Kendricks.

"The Crown Prosecutor won't agree to proceed," said Brigham. His voice was a soft whisper, and confusion was all over his face.

"I'm going for lunch," said Mary.

* * *

Lisa sat in her armchair, her head in her hands. Despite her intense relief at being released from a cell and returning home, the shock and fear of her arrest remained in her, filling her body with sickness.

"I told you I would take care of the situation," said the familiar voice of Vanth.

Lisa looked up to see the image seated across from her. It gave her no comfort.

"I can't keep going like this," she muttered. "I want out. This is no life to lead."

"You have no choice," said the demon. "Once you owned all three cursed items, your destiny was fixed. You have only one reason to exist, that is to kill Tarquinia. The need to kill others is simply the force within you before you started. It was there from birth."

"And there is no escape for me?"

"None."

The demon vanished. Lisa was overcome with grief.

Chapter 26 – An Old Life Revisited

Without thinking, Lisa reverted to the dark, hopeless period she had inhabited on returning to England and being told her inevitable future in an Etruscan Hell. She slept most of the day, watched television at night, fell into regular bouts of intensive tears and let herself go to pieces. She washed rarely, hardly knew what clothes she wore when she eventually got out of bed and mentally retreated into a dull, shapeless world she hardly touched.

Then, as before, she began to resurface. Waking up soon after dawn, she realised how badly her bed smelled, herself the same, what a mess the house was. Swearing at herself, she got up, showered for the first time in a week and found fresh clothes in her closet.

The day was spent in a blizzard of activity as he cleaned the house, ran the vacuum cleaner over the floors and spent over two hours just cleaning up the horrific, smelly mess in the kitchen. She could not remember what she had eaten the last two or three weeks, but there was no food in the refrigerator. Pausing the final stage, her parent's bedroom, Lisa instead found her purse and handbag, extracted the car keys and drove to the coffee shop in town where she recalled a full breakfast menu was available.

When the waitress approached, Lisa tried to order coffee and eggs on toast, but found that her voice was almost non-functional, having not spoken since her short conversation with the demon after her release from prison. Smiling apologetically, she pointed at her choice. The waitress understood and a little while later, Lisa attacked the food energetically.

On her return home, she decided she had to make the final effort with the house. She had not entered her parent's bedroom the whole time she had been back in England, almost overwhelmed with anger at the memory of her last meeting with them when both had died, one of them at her own hands. But now she opened the door and walked in. The sight was unsettling.

The room was perfectly neat and tidy, as left by the previous tenants. The bed was made to hospital standards, but the pillows were covered with dust. So too, were the bedside cabinets and the lampshades for the bedside lights. Forcing herself, Lisa stripped the bed and carried the sheets and pillowcases down to the laundry. She came back with the vacuum cleaner and spent twenty minutes restoring the carpet, returning it to the blue and red colour pattern that was lost under the heavy dust.

Finally, she went to the wardrobes. They were empty, as she expected, but not entirely so. As Hollier had told her, there was a large green cabin trunk on one side of the cabinet. She pulled the box out into the room. It was unlocked. Feeling some trepidation, she unlatched the two latches dand swung the heavy lid open.

The contents were unexpected. The first thing she saw was a large doll. It had blonde hair, the traditional rosy cheeks of a child's doll of many years ago and was dressed in a long blue dress.

"Betsy," exclaimed Lisa and broke into a fit of weeping. This had been her inseparable companion for as long as she could remember until she had started high school and deliberately put away her childhood possessions. She picked up the doll and held it closely.

It was ten minutes later that she remembered to examine the rest of the contents. There were four small pictures in frames, and she recognised herself and her parents in all of them, showing her at different ages. She guessed she was from four to eight and her parents seemed not to age at all. Below the framed photographs were four small dresses, and she saw that they were the dresses she was wearing in the pictures, growing larger as she aged further. She was startled to see that her parents had kept these things. There were several notebooks at the bottom of the box, but Lisa felt too shocked to explore further.

Emotionally drained, Lisa returned downstairs, still holding Betsy and sat in her armchair, rocking back and forth as memories of childhood flooded into her mind. She stayed that way until dusk fell, becoming increasingly agitated as she recalled the life she had led since arranging to kill a homeless derelict together with Pete and Dylan.

"I don't want to do that anymore," said a little girl's voice in her mind. She knew it was herself, little Lisa, aged about seven or eight.

"I won't," she said aloud and resolved to change everything. That night, she slept with Betsy in her arms and tried to remember how she had been before death became her preoccupation. It wasn't easy. Her dreams were badly disturbed by soft voices that somehow she knew were those of her younger self. When she could work out what she was saying, the words were, "I don't want to keep doing this."

She woke up seriously fatigued and stressed.

The following three weeks were a nightmare. Spending most of the time sitting in the lounge room, cradling Betsy and stroking the doll's hair, Lisa reviewed her earlier years, startled by how clearly she remembered some of those times.

Her best friend, she recalled, was Annabelle. Lisa couldn't remember her second name, but she clearly saw in her mind the slightly-built child aged seven, the same age as Lisa. The both had a favourite doll, Annabelle's was a red-head called Trudie, usually dressed in a stylish pantsuit, though some of the girls' favourite playtimes was changing the clothing of the dolls. Trudie sometimes wore an elegant ballgown, sometimes a royal blue track suit. Lisa's favourite styles for Betsy were always pretty dresses, always with lace borders. They talked about their parents a lot. Lisa always expressed how much she loved her father, but was never close to her mother, she seemed distant, sometimes even hostile. Annabelle had no such problems, she adored both parents equally.

They would take walks into nearby Leyland Woods and pick flowers.

Lisa jerked upright, a scream rising in her throat as she saw images of the woods, even the grassy clearing where Pete and Dylan had garrotted Jake in front of her. It was the same clearing where they had waited before killing the old lady.

"I don't want to keep doing this," she said aloud. It was the voice of seven-year-old Lisa. She fell back in her armchair, weeping loudly, hugging Betsy to her as if she would never let go.

Annabelle's family moved to Canada when she was eleven and the hole in Lisa's life was never properly filled. Lisa entered puberty more than a year before anyone else in the class and this caused a rift between her and the other girls. Her body developed curves like a teenager, attracting the attention of the more senior boys in the school. It excited her but caused jealousy and hostile comments from the girls who increasingly moved away from her. She spent more and more time in the company of boys four, even five years older than her and she enjoyed that, though constantly fending off physical moves on her became a constant irritation.

Jake was a particularly attractive young man, and she allowed greater intimacy with him.

Once more, Lisa jerked out of her reveries, a scream escaping from her. She knew that she had been happy in those days, even with the isolation caused by her maturity. No visions of deaths of old men, blood spattering over her overalls and recalling the satisfaction she got from the killing. She had never thought of killing, never thought of leading two boys into murder.

"I don't want to do that again," said the voice of seven-year-old Lisa.

"You don't have a choice," said the demon. She was standing behind Lisa but moved to take the other armchair. "I have told you so often, this is your destiny. As a young Vulci girl, once you had put on all three of the cursed ornaments, your fate was dictated. There is no escape."

Lisa was trembling, but something in her welcomed the sight of the demon. It recalled the flush of warmth, of power and pride when she wore the necklace, the ring and the bracelet, the wild exultation she experienced when she killed a Tarquinian, a flush of power, so much more fulfilling than killing any other mortal.

"Go and get them," ordered the image in the other seat.

Needing no further urging, Lisa went to the safe, opened it and donned all three ornaments.

Immediately, she felt as if she were a goddess, the power in her could overwhelm the world and an old desire raced back into her body. She needed to kill, anybody, not necessarily a Tarquinian, just another human. She desperately needed to deal a killing blow with a knife, see the pain and anguish in the other face as the light died in the eyes and the body slumped to the ground and blood rushed out of the gashes she had caused.

No little girl's voice could be heard.

Lisa was a supreme killer.

Feeling no need of the campervan again, Lisa had sold it through an auction system, not meeting the buyer face to face. She replaced it at a large, used-car market with a nondescript, second-hand, grey sedan, looking for something as unremarkable as possible.

One evening, she dressed in neat but conventional clothing, nothing like the man-catching ensemble she had worn as a blonde, wore a black, short-haired wig and drove nearly a hundred kilometres to a larger town. Entering the club that she had identified on the internet, she bought a vodka at the bar and waited. It wasn't too long before the bait worked.

"Haven't seen you here before," said the tall, slender man as he settled down beside her.

She smiled. "Possibly because I haven't been here before," she responded in her best seductive tones.

It didn't take long before her suggestion to take a break was received with enthusiasm and they left in her car. Three days earlier, Lisa had scouted out the area and found the perfect spot. Now she stopped off the road, behind a line of trees and she invited the man out to the grassy section she had found.

Seconds later, she plunged her knife into the man's throat, repeated the blow into his heart and watched in delight as the shock in his face faded, his eyes closed, and his body slumped.

"God, I needed that," she murmured. She returned to the car, took out the overalls she had previously packed away and put it on to cover up the blood spatters on her dress, followed up with new rubber gloves, then carefully drove out of the hidden space, back to the road and the two-hour drive home. There she packed all her clothes, the wig and the overalls into the incinerator, took a long hot shower including a careful shampoo and settled down with a glass of wine before the television. She felt relaxed and complete.

There was no sound from little Lisa.

Chapter 27 – Conflict

Lisa Kendricks woke up screaming.

Sitting upright, she felt sweat running down her body, along her legs and in her hair. Trembling, she tried to stay still, struggling to remember what had caused the nightmare.

"Please," said the voice of seven-year-old Lisa. It was louder, stronger than before and could almost have come from elsewhere in the room. "I don't want to do this any more." Lisa opened her eyes. Her younger self was sitting in the chair across from her bed.

"We have to," grated Lisa. "I'm cursed, I have no options."

"We mustn't," said the child. "We'll go to hell. I don't want to go to hell. Please stop."

"We're going to hell, anyway." Lisa's voice was harsh, frightened. "I'm cursed."

"Please stop," said the child. "Maybe we can still be saved if we stop now."

"No chance," said Lisa, tears rising to her eyes. "If I stop, I'll go insane."

"Lisa, you're already insane," said the child. "Don't you realise it?"

Lisa screamed and switched on the light. The child vanished.

"I'm not insane, I'm cursed," said Lisa, got up, threw off the sweat-soaked clothes and had another shower. The rest of the night, she spent before the television, unable to sleep again, sometimes sensing her younger self struggling to be heard again. Sometime before dawn, she finally fell asleep, but it was a restless, frightened sleep.

The whole of the next day, she was badly fatigued, her body aching with the need to sleep, but unable to. Finally, she did what she knew was her only outlet. She opened the safe, put on the ornaments and felt the rush of power, hatred and bloodlust sweep through her again.

Little Lisa was silent. Adult Lisa finally fell asleep.

* * *

After three days, Lisa felt settled enough to return to her parent's bedroom and look at the cabin trunk she had pulled out of the closet. There were four books of notes, written in thick, hardcover diaries. Curiously, Lisa opened each of them and saw that two were in her mother's handwriting, two in her father's. She began reading her mother's notes and it was not long before she experienced deep dismay.

September, 1995, first week at High School. My first History lesson and what a shock this was. The stupid teacher said we'd look at World War Two and that seemed okay, because my Dad talks a lot about it. He always said Britain and America fought on the wrong side, we should have allied with Germany to destroy those communists in Russia. And here's this teacher saying Germany was ruled by fascists and had done dreadful things to people all over Europe and killed over six million Jews. My Dad says that stuff about the Holocaust was all rubbish, Hitler only killed a million or so Jews and he should have wiped them out because Jews killed Christ and they're nothing but crooks running banks to steal as much as they can. I'm going to tell my Dad about this and he's a very powerful man who runs a large corporation. I know he told me once that he won't hire Jews or Blacks.

"Good grief," said Lisa. "Mother was a Nazi-admirer?" She turned a few pages and read another section.

March, 1998. I did an essay for the history course. I got Dad to help me a bit and I wrote a really good analysis of how Hitler rescued Germany in the thirties. He was really a great man. He rebuilt the economy and opened up millions of jobs for Germans, mostly by building up the military. Getting rid of those Jews was a great help, because they just stifled Germany's economy, but they were more help being recruited as labour into German industries. The teacher called me in, gave me a right talking to and failed my paper. I told Dad about her and he's going to get her fired.

"I knew Grandad was rich," muttered Lisa. "I never realised the influence he had, or that he was such a Nazi. This is horrible, it's embarrassing. I hope nobody knows about this." She pushed a few pages along and read another section.

July, 2010. Dad told me not to talk about Hitler and the Nazis again, people wouldn't understand. So I avoided the topic and when I got into Grade 11 and concentrated on History as my major topic, I spent most time on British Empire and American topics. I'm getting good marks, just as well that Hitler-hating bitch got fired and couldn't affect anything I did. I'll go to University in a couple of years and aim at a degree in History and then a doctorate. Dad will make sure I get accepted, he always gets what he wants. I suppose it's easy when you have a few hundred million pounds in the bank.

"No wonder I never liked you, Mother," said Lisa. "How the hell did you end up married to a nice man like Dad?"

September, 2002. First year at University! I really didn't think my grades were good enough, but Dad said he had a talk with the school Principal and agreed to pull some strings and here I am, doing a degree in History with sociology and economics as secondaries. Dad warned me that at some stage, the course would examine the rise of Germany and Hitler in the thirties and World War Two and I had to just shut up and never object to what the material said. He said it was standard policy to show Germany as the wicked enemy in the war, and nobody could challenge the

Holocaust. If I wanted to get my degree, I just had to keep quiet on the subject.

May, 2005. At last, a social life. I went to a party the other night and chatted up several guys. They kept staring down my neckline – and I must admit, I'd dressed to have that effect - and I had a few good snogs with several of them. But one of them seemed particularly nice. He's Robert Kendricks and he's a graduate student in archaeology. I can't understand what's interesting in digging up ancient buildings and graves and stuff, but he's got a great body, and I've enjoyed the snogs we've had. His hands aren't as busy as those other blokes, which is a relief, but things have been heating up a bit the last few times.

Laughing at this image of her cold, unemotional and distant mother having a sex life, Lisa advanced further along the book.

June, 2009. We'd finally done the deed back in January, during the holidays in the first year, when we went for a dirty weekend in Wales. It had been a bit painful at first, but Robert was very gentle, and it became okay after the first few times. I've no idea why the other girls I know rave about it so much, though. We took all the usual precautions. Despite that, big news – I'm pregnant. I told Robert and he said it was my choice what to do, but he'd support me whatever I decided. But he hoped I'd decide to keep it, he'd always wanted a child. I told him I wanted to get rid of it, I couldn't handle having a kid when I started my PhD program. So we decided to go home and tell my parents. That was a mistake. Dad hit the roof, started screaming at Robert and then at me when I told him I wanted an abortion. He got all religious, really fanatical and yelled that I'd be damned to hell if I did that, abortion was against Christ, blah, blah, blah. He told Robert that he had to marry me, or he'd destroy his career, so we had no choice.

"You wanted to abort me, Mother?" said Lisa. "No wonder you've always resented me, never shown any warmth at all. And that's why Dad and I were always so close, he really loved me. You sure as hell didn't." Lisa pulled open the book near the end to see what happened when she was a child. The result shook he beyond belief.

February, 2010. It's been a horrible year. I grew as fat as an elephant, and I agreed with the university to delay my doctoral studies for a year. I hated being pregnant and I sure as hell won't do it again. Of course, Dad helped, supplied me with a full-time nurse and all the domestic help I wanted. God knows how I would have coped without that. Then the worst part, actually giving birth. I screamed like hell until they gave me a jab of something, and I only have hazy memories of the next hour or so. When they put this little bundle in my arms, I didn't get all gooey the way women are supposed to do. I felt nothing really, just a bit resentful of what she had caused me. And I had to feed it also, and I found that uncomfortable, didn't get all gooey the way women are supposed to feel. Dad said he'd provide full time help at home and after three months, I was able to start my studies. So I rarely saw the kid. Robert got all clucky about her and spent as much time as he could at my place with her.

"So that explains it," said Lisa aloud. "No wonder you were such a cold, uncaring old cow, you never wanted me." She felt tears coming to her eyes, together with a wave of anger at the way her mother had treated her in her most fragile years. The next section she found shocked her badly.

December, 2015. I killed that bitch of a teacher. I saw her in the mall and followed her out. She didn't recognise me of course, I was only eleven when she spouted that ugly anti-German crap into our ears and now I'm a full-grown woman. So I watched her reach her car and drive off and I noted the number. I went to the mall every day for the next two weeks after that and looked for her car and finally saw her again. This time, I was prepared. I had parked near her car and when the bitch drove off, I followed her until she drove into the garage of a house just a few kilometres away. I watched the house for a few hours, then again on three more days and never saw anybody else going in or out. I planned the event carefully. Rather than buy a set of overalls, and risk being remembered at the store as a woman buying the mostly masculine item, I made a set myself, it was easy with my sewing machine. I've watched enough episodes of cop shows on the tv to know how to hide evidence, so I made covers for my shoes, found my thin, leather gloves, took a carving knife from the kitchen and drove out to the bitch's house at about nine at night. I parked away from the house, then went and knocked on the door. As soon as she opened it, I slammed the door wide open, walked in and drove the knife into her chest. I stayed only long enough to watch her drop to the floor, then made a rapid exit to my car. It was quite dark and there was nobody around as I stripped off my overalls and shoe covers and drove home. Once inside, I pushed the outside clothes into the fireplace, poured a vodka and sat by the tv for a couple of hours. I felt great.

Lisa was stunned. She had never seen any evidence of warmth or empathy in her mother, nor her sister, Lisa's aunt, but a killer? And the way she had used to hide her involvement was exactly as Lisa had used for her first murders back as a young girl. "Is this where I get it from?" she muttered aloud. "And for God's sake, Mum, why did you write this down where somebody might find it?" She thought for a moment. "Ah yes, you privileged cow, you knew daddy would always protect you, didn't you? What the hell happened next?" She leafed forward and found the answer.

The cops came early the following morning. They said somebody had seen me enter the house just as the hallway light came on for a few seconds. They had followed me back to my car, noted the number and then called the police. The woman cop said they had found a small smear of blood on the door of the car, checked it and found it to be the blood of the dead woman. I was arrested and taken to the cop shop. When I was able to make a telephone call, I called my Dad, and he took charge. He called a real barracuda of a lawyer, and I was out on bail an hour later. Dad was furious, but said he'd make sure I didn't face jail time.

Unable to think clearly, Lisa turned the page.

I went to see the lawyer with my dad. The lawyer said not to worry, he'd get me off. I'd have to be in the court, but I would not be asked to speak. The next day, the trial was set. I really don't know how it happened, but the jury said I was not guilty. I have no idea how the lawyer did it, but Dad said he was the best in the country. Robert knew all about it, of course, but agreed never to speak about it when Dad told him he'd never work again if he did. A week later, I heard that the woman who had been the only witness had been found dead in the river. I never asked Dad if he had anything to do with it, but I'm pretty sure he did.

"Good god, my mother was a killer. And I was right, daddy really did get you off." Lisa felt sick. Was this the same killer instinct in herself, the one characteristic she had inherited from her mother? She put the book down. She had no urge to look at her father's notes.

Chapter 28 - Father's History

It took Lisa a week before she found the courage to open her father's notebook, frightened of what revelations she could encounter. But nothing hit her in the opening pages, just a surprise that her father only started his diary at University.

September, 1990. First week at University! This is magic, finally getting away from my parents' smoke-filled slum and finding freedom. I had saved almost all the money I had made working holiday jobs since I was twelve, so I was able to rent a decent apartment in a house owned by a nice, elderly couple, Les and Freda. My own kitchen, would you believe, so I'm able to experiment with cooking stuff that doesn't taste of cigarette ash as it had at home. First few days were mainly social stuff, a gathering of Freshers from all faculties and one for the History department. A bit scary, all those gorgeous girls around. I'm not used to that, my school was an all-boys place, and I have to admit I'm a bit useless in that department.

Still, I'm sure History was a good choice, and I've opted for a minor in Archaeology, something that has always interested me.

"No wonder I was never taken to meet my grandparents," said Lisa aloud. "Dad never talked about them and when he did go and see them, very rarely, neither I nor mum were asked to go along. And as for Mum's parents, I sure as hell wouldn't have wanted to meet them, certainly not her father. Anyway, nice to see that Dad seemed to be a normal human being. Anyway, let's move along." She opened the book at a random place and read further.

April, 1998, Graduation with First Class Honours! YAY! And I got even better grades in archaeology. That dig we did in Tel Aviv probably did it for me, some of the scrolls I found and was able to translate from Greek and Aramaic were discussed all over the world, I even got interviewed on the BBC and a couple of American networks talked to me as well. So I've opted for my doctorate in archaeology, rather than History. And another milestone – I'm embarrassed that it took so long, but I finally surrendered my virginity. It was a party to celebrate graduation, and I got together with Gita, she of the amazing body and waist-length hair, who had been in my class from the start. Not quite sure how it happened, but we ended up in my place after midnight, Les and Freda were well asleep and we got down to business rather enthusiastically. But that was it for the affair. Gita had already accepted a lecturer position at the University of Toronto and left three days later. I got a wonderful offer from Oxford, and I'll start in August.

"Well done, Dad," said Lisa with a laugh. "I often wondered about your sex life. Sounds like it was better late than never. Let's see what happens."

The next few random readings discussed the lecturer's life in a world-famous university and reviews of a few archaeology digs around the world, but she stumbled on one that struck a nerve.

When they told me we were going to the old world of the Etruscans, something struck a light in me. I had always been fascinated by this strange civilisation of which so little was known and yet had left some powerful marks on the world. I could hardly wait until we left to spend the summer break in northern Italy.

This was the strangest thing. As soon as we entered the structure known as "The Tomb of the Sun and the Moon" as it was referenced in one of the few translated carved words on a stone in the region, I felt a strange sense of homecoming. It was bizarre, almost as if I had been here many times. The Etruscans buried their entire families and descendants in these large structures and there have been a number of invaluable and wonderful findings. This tomb was for one of the ruling families of Etruria, known as the "League of Twelve," and was identified as the Vulci family. My team will be here for six weeks, and I doubt I will want to think about anything else in that time.

"That must have been weird, Dad. What a shame that you never knew that was your family heritage. You were a Vulci and you could never know it."

One amazing carving caused a shiver down my spine. Little is known about Etruscan religion, except that it had several gods and quite a few demons. The carving we found deep in the tomb was of a female demon. She wears a short, pleated skirt and her breasts are bound in straps. She carries a hammer and a torch. One of the language experts has identified her as Vanth, the Demon of Death, one of the few female demons of the Etruscan religion. Her role is mainly that of escorting the dead to the Underworld.

Lisa gasped in dismay. This was the demon who had been communicating with her almost since she had first donned the ornaments from the Vulci tomb. Was it she who would take Lisa down to Hell when she died? Trembling, Lisa closed the notebook and fell into a tight foetal position, overwhelmed by fear.

It took another week for Lisa to find the courage to open her father's notebook again. One of first sections she opened to was fascinating.

May, 2008 — went to another of those faculty parties. Since working on my doctorate, I haven't been to many of those, finding them a bit immature. Over the years at University, I have dated only a few girls, and they seem to cool off when I discuss my work. Perhaps I'm a bit too passionate about it. But this evening, I met a girl and struck up a more interesting conversation than exchanging our star signs. Rachel Bellingen, she's called, she's the daughter of some multi-millionaire corporate executive and seemed a little frightened of him. She has a sister, her only sibling. Anyway, one thing led to another, and I found myself engaged in a fairly passionate session in one of the reading rooms. Actually, I must admit, it wasn't as exciting as the wild groping session with the amazing Gita some years earlier, but after a lengthy celibate period, I was able to settle for it. Somehow, she seemed keen on maintaining the affair.

November, 2009. The thing with Rachel seems to have progressed in conventional fashion and we finally went off for a dirty weekend in Wales. She assured me that she had been on the pill for over a year, and we had indulged often enough in that period, so it was alarming when she told me yesterday that she was pregnant. She thinks that perhaps she missed taking the pill that once. I told her I'll support her whatever she chooses to do, but she said firmly she'll get an abortion. She said she wants to go home to tell the family and wants me to go with her. That scares me a bit, but I've agreed to go.

December, 2009. Ten days before Christmas, Rachel and I arrived at the family mansion in Surrey. A palatial bloody place, quite intimidating, reflecting enormous wealth and very little taste. But if the house was intimidating, her father was terrifying. Bellingen was a large man in every dimension, very loud and incapable of hearing any opinion that differed from his. When Rachel told his she had decided on an abortion, he exploded. Turned out he was one of those rabid Christian fundamentalists that they call

Christian Nationalists in the USA. We got a long ferocious rant about how God didn't tolerate abortion, it was an insult to Christ and no way in the world would she have one. Somehow, the rant veered into a rave about how the Jews had killed Christ and were the servants of Satan, responsible for all the ills of the world.

We stayed there overnight, and it was a nightmare, literally. I was shown to a tiny bedroom that was normally used as a storeroom, and I retreated there gratefully after an awful dinner during which Bellingen continued his ravings when he wasn't eating like a pig at the trough. Nobody else got in a word, the wife, a mousy little person looked terrified the whole time, Rachel's younger sister, Angela seemed to have detached herself entirely and appeared to be looking into another world the whole time. The only positive thing was the occasional sympathetic look I got from the two servants who said not a word but efficiently served the food and removed the plates. No wine was served. I slept badly, wondering what the hell I had got into.

The morning came with another hammer blow.

"You'll marry her, right?" bellowed Bellingen as soon as I appeared. "Because if you don't, I'll destroy you, understand? Whatever this stupid archaeology thing is, you'll be dead to the profession. Got me?"

All I could do was nod and we left as soon as we possibly could.

"And that was him on a good day," said Rachel as we drove out of the imposing gates. That was the only laugh I could muster the whole time.

"Holy shit!" exploded Lisa as she reached the end of that entry. "Now I know why I never got to meet my grandparents. Dad, you poor bastard, I never knew how bad it had been. I could tell there was no real affection between you two, but I never knew what you had gone through."

She opened the book a few pages on and continued reading.

June, 2010. I must admit, married life with Rachel is not good. I was exiled to a second bedroom quite early on after she complained I snored. I concentrated more and more on my work and Rachel did the same. She was less successful, never getting tenure, remaining only as an assistant professor. Financially we're fine, her father makes sure she needs nothing. While he had no interest in seeing Lisa, his granddaughter, he kept putting money into her school fund and we always have enough money for vacations, clothes and the mortgage, which I paid off quickly.

As a professor of some reputation, I had some positive characteristics. I have realised rather late in life that I'm not a bad-looking bloke and I've learnt the art of entertaining conversation. I think if I'd realised this some years ago and not suffered from the lack of self-confidence, my social life would have been much more stimulating that it had been. So it has been nice to allow myself to have attractive women become attached to me on occasions. Rachel was totally distant, I think she resents Lisa and has little to do with her. But fortunately, we can afford a full-time nanny and that is who is bringing up my delightful daughter. I spend as much time as I can with her also.

September, 2014 - A major shock this week. My current lady, Audrey, has just told me she's pregnant. She plans to keep the child and she's independently wealthy from a grandfather's bequest, so she's making no demands on me. In fact, she says she hopes I'll visit whenever I can. I intend to, the idea of having more kids, even if I can't acknowledge them is too good.

July, 2015. I have twin daughters, Heather and Janet! I went to the hospital and saw these tiny mites, just a week old and I love them totally. I hope that one day they can meet their half-sister, Lisa.

"Dad, you old rogue!" exclaimed Lisa. "I never knew you had it in you! Half-sisters! Bloody amazing. I'm going to have to see if I can trace them." Feeling much happier than she had, Lisa put the notebook away and went to bed. The following day, she returned to her father's history. The first thing she read was startling.

Rachel just told me about how she had killed the teacher she'd known in High School. I was so shocked,

I could barely speak for a while. And she jumped in ahead of anything I wanted to say. She reminded me that she had been tried and found not guilty of murder, so if I tried talking about this, her father would sue me to bankruptcy for libel. So how do I deal with this? I've taken to locking my bedroom door, I have no idea if she would consider killing me because I know about it. I'm even more frightened for Lisa. It has always been obvious that Rachel has no love for her daughter, obviously resents her for causing problems in her career. Could she somehow facilitate killing her own daughter? I don't think the idea is too preposterous, it's clear she has no human empathy and warmth. I also know that if I tried leaving and taking Lisa with me, her father would seek retribution, and I can't see any limit to what he would do. All I can do is behave as if everything was normal, maintain a sociable if distant relationship with my wife and stay apart as much as possible.

"Good God, was I so at risk?" murmured Lisa. "Could my mother have killed me out of resentment? I think it was possible, now that I know more about her and her awful family. I think it was lucky that Dad killed her when he did. Another few years, and I can well imagine Mum getting really shitty as she grew older and I started having a life as a teenager. That's when she could have just lost it and killed me somehow. Finding those two books has been an incredible shock. What else am I going to find?"

July, 2017. I found another excuse to be away for a couple of days and visited Audrey and the twins again in Farnborough. In some ways, it was heart-breaking. Audrey at thirty is a lovely, graceful, warm woman and the twins are a delight. At two years old, they are typical toddlers, enough energy to power a small town, and all three of them are so close. Audrey has not found another relationship, she thinks most men are scared of getting entangled with a woman with children. This is sad, because the twins so obviously would love to have a father figure. They have latched onto me, barely moving away from me at all times, sitting on my knees and chatting at full speed. I can't help but think how different life would be married to Audrey and having these wonderful two kiddies as my daughters. I find myself occasionally fantasising of leaving Rachel and taking Lisa with me, marrying Audrey and leading a truly fulfilling life. But I made my bed, now I must lie on it.

"Oh Dad, it's what you deserved," said Lisa. "It's tragic that it never became possible. I had no option but to kill you when I did, it would have been too risky to leave you alive, knowing what I had become. And it saved you from discovering that not only was your wife a killer, but you daughter was even worse, a serial killer who had lost count of the murders she had committed."

Chapter 29 – Finding Her Father's Past

After two days of deep thought about her father's past, Lisa decided to follow up on her earlier idea about tracing the woman, Audrey and her two children. She had no idea of how to start looking for them, so decided to call in a specialist, and after searching through the Internet, called a local Private Investigator. That afternoon, he arrived at her house.

"I'm Terry Carstairs," he said when Lisa opened the front door to the sound of the bell. She saw a man in his forties, dressed in a blue blazer and grey flannels and a full head of jet-black hair.

"Come on in," she said and led him to the lounge room. She had called in an industrial cleaning company the week before and had instructed the team of four young people to give the house the most intensive clean-up they could. After three days, the house looked quite liveable again.

Carstairs took the seat she indicated to him and sat still while he was obviously examined carefully. Finally, Lisa smiled and signalled her approval.

"My father was Professor Robert Kendricks," Lisa began. "He was the professor of archaeology at Oxford for some years, but he died a few years ago. I know that at one point he was became involved with a woman called Audrey, second name unknown, no idea whether she was on the university staff or not. The last I knew, she lived in Farnborough and has twin daughters, Heather and Janet, born in July, 2020. Dad visited them two years later, while Audrey still lived at the same place. I have no other information. Do you think you could trace her?"

Carstairs put down the notebook in which he had been carefully writing down the information.

"I've had easier assignments," he said. "This certainly presents difficulties, but I've also had harder jobs. Let's discuss fees."

Twenty minutes later, Carstairs left, promising weekly progress reports.

"Reasonable progress," said Carstairs over the telephone after six days. "I talked to the University HR Department, they knew your father well and named several of his friends. Some of those were on staff at some time, so they had their addresses. I talked to five of those and three of them remember Audrey and her passionate affair with your father. They all envied him, they agreed she was drop-dead gorgeous and a really sweet person. Her name then was Ashfield. None of them kept in touch with her after your father died."

"Excellent," said Lisa. "What's next?"

"I'll be in Farnborough in a couple of hours. First stop the Council Rates office. I'll get back to you."

"Thank you," said Lisa.

A week later, the phone rang again.

"Am I good or am I good?" said Carstairs. The laughter in his voice was obvious, something Lisa found most attractive.

"You've found Audrey?"

"Damn right. Still at the same address in Farnborough with the twins."

"That's amazing, Terry. I think you can claim that you are really *very* good."

"Thank you, Ma'am. I think we're done. My bill is in the post."

"I promise to pay it, with a bonus."

* * *

"Is that Audrey Ashfield?"

"It is. Who's calling?"

"Audrey, this will a shock to you. My name is Lisa Kendricks.."

"Oh my God, Robert's daughter?"

"Yes, I am. Robert mentioned me?"

"Mentioned you? Good lord, you were the main talking point most of the time. He obviously adored you."

"Can I come and visit? I'd love to see you, dad wrote very lovingly about you and the girls."

"You'd better. I'll get Heather and Janet to be here."

"Saturday morning okay? I'm only two hours away"

"Perfect. I think I'm going to cry."

"Me too."

* * *

Lisa stopped the car outside the small bungalow on the outskirts of Farnborough. It was neat, freshly painted with a well-kept garden at the front, a mix of coloured roses along the front fence. Taking a deep breath, she got out of the car and walked up to the front door. It opened before she was able to press the bell.

The woman in front of her looked in her forties, very trim, short red hair over an unlined face. She was about the same height as Lisa and displayed a neat, well-proportioned body. Lisa knew she was in her late fifties, but that was not in the least obvious.

The two women stared at each other. The smile of welcome that had been on Audrey's face died almost immediately, replaced by an anxious look.

"Lisa?" said Audrey. She stepped back a little, as if frightened by what she saw.

"Yes. This is wonderful to see you." Lisa felt a wave of concern. *Why was this woman not as pleased to see her as she had expected?*

"Come in," said Audrey and stood aside to let Lisa walk through into the short corridor. Straight ahead, she could see French Windows framing more neat gardens.

Lisa walked into the spacious lounge to see two girls standing, obviously waiting for her. Both showed expressions of delight, but to Lisa's dismay, they faded as she walked in.

Audrey followed her and joined her daughters. All three continued to look at Lisa, all with hostile, almost frightened faces.

"What is wrong?" Lisa asked. "You seem terribly upset about something."

"You're frightening us," replied Audrey. "I don't know what it is, but there's something awful about you."

"I'm Robert Kendricks' daughter," said Lisa, her throat becoming tense in the wave of fear that radiated from all of the women. "I'm the half-sister of you, Heather and Janet. Why am I so frightening?"

"I don't know," replied Audrey. "But you are."

The twins had moved close together and were holding hands. The fear in them had worsened and both girls were white faced.

"Lisa, whatever has gone wrong, you can't stay," said Audrey. Tears were rolling down her cheeks. "I always wanted to meet Robert's daughter and I know how badly he wanted you to meet the girls. But there's something terribly wrong, we're all terrified, just why I have no idea."

"Nor have I," said Lisa. But she did know. The killing lust in her was now showing and radiating from her. She knew she had to leave.

"I'm so sorry," she said. "But at least I have seen you."

She turned and walked out of the room, opened the front door and left. As she sat in the car, she burst into heavy tears. It was a while before she started the car and drove away.

For two more weeks, Lisa tended to break into fitful weeping sessions as she recalled the meeting with her father's second family. She had so much wanted to meet them, but the meeting had been nothing like she had imagined. She had never realised that the dreadful killing urge within her might be seen by others.

At one point, she remembered the series of failed relationships she had experienced when young men had been initially attracted to her but had eased away after a period of usually no more than two weeks. They had seen the same killing urge in her that Audrey and the twins had seen.

"My god, what have I become?" she sobbed into her hands. There was no good answer to that.

Chapter 30 - the Curse Continues

Reading the histories of her parents made Lisa sink into a deeply introspective period. Some of the time was spent in sadness at the difficult and unfulfilling life of her father, with profound regrets that she had felt herself forced by circumstances to kill him. She wondered about her mother and her mother's family, such an ugly bunch, full of admiration for Nazis and their bullying, overbearing approach to the world. How much of that, especially her mother's murder of a teacher because she disagreed with her, had been in her own character? Had she become this serial murderer because she was like her mother or was it all the Vulci curse she had taken on when she donned the ornaments cursed by a demon?

She realised that she had been touched by her father's obvious unhappiness and yearning for a life with Audrey and the two children he had fathered with her. The disastrous meeting with Audrey and the twins made that feeling worse. Slowly, that thought became predominant and Lisa began to sense some emotional and physical urges that had been dormant for a while. A week later, she found a new disguise, a flaming red wig and a set of clothing much like she had worn when she had gone to the club and picked out a victim for killing. The skirt was even shorter, the blouse cut deeper and the heels even higher.

Some research on the computer found a likely venue, a club with a popular reputation for atmosphere and music in a town just two hours away. She packed the outfit into a bag, wore jeans and sweater and drove off. Stopping in a restaurant just a few blocks from the club, she changed in the washroom and emerged in her eye-catching new personality, getting considerable attention as she walked through the restaurant to the exit.

The plan worked perfectly. At the club, she had a collection of men vying for attention. Picking the one she decided had the best body and good looks, she was able to talk with him over a drink and found that he had all the intellectual attributes she sought. Killing was not in the plan this night, something different was the key factor.

Eventually, she ended up at his home, and the sex was intensive and long lasting. She allowed herself to stay for nearly three hours before she left the bed, got dressed and softly let herself out of the house while the man was asleep. She was certain things had gone to plan. Just over two hours later, she was home again.

* * *

"I suppose you're going to order me to have an abortion again?" Lisa felt strangely defiant facing the demon. She knew well that the frightening woman seated in front of her could cause a miscarriage at any time, but there was something about how she felt that steeled her nerve.

To her surprise, Vanth smiled and looked almost human. She was not dressed in her Etruscan Angel of

Death garb, but wore a simple business suit and could be almost any middle-aged woman.

"No," said Vanth. "We want you to have this child."

"You do? Why? Last time you ordered the abortion immediately with no discussion allowed. What's different this time?"

"This time, we know the child will continue the mission."

"The mission? To kill Tarquinia? Why is that important to you?"

The demon smiled again. "The mission has never been simply to kill Tarquinia. It has been to kill in significant numbers. The Underworld has been lacking in inmates since the world's religions moved away from the Etruscan world. You have served our purpose well and provided many new souls for us."

Lisa felt horrified.

"So you used the Vulci curse for your own purposes? You used my curse to kill far more than just Tarquinia?"

"You think that demons would show honesty and some sort of business integrity? Are you such a fool, Lisa?"

Lisa felt her body turn cold. "And you will force my child to continue this path?"

"Oh yes. She will be perfect. She has your lust to kill and the Vulci curse will increase that."

"She? I will have a daughter? And the curse will continue with her?"

"That is so. The power of the artifacts will continue, regardless of whether she wears them."

Lisa felt a flood of torment. Some part of her was delighted at the idea of having a daughter, but it was conflicted with the knowledge of what that daughter would be.

* * *

Three weeks passed and Lisa slowly lost all memory of the last conversation with Vanth, the Angel of Death. She heard no more from the voice of a twelve-year-old child trying to remind her of who she really was. Instead, the killing urge grew stronger again and with it, the frustration of being unable to find another member of the Tarquinia to slaughter.

One evening, she sat before her mirror and donned the gold necklace, the ring and the copper bracelet and once more felt the rush of power and the urge to kill flood into her body. Every muscle in her hands tingled at the memory of plunging a knife into a human body and she could almost taste the blood in her mouth. She watched as the image in the mirror evolved from the young woman she was and became the face of a much older woman. It was unnerving for Lisa to see the image display lines around the mouth, deep shadows around the eyes, greying hair and an expression of anger and discontent making the image ugly and repellent.

"Yes, that is what you are becoming," said the voice of the Angel of Death behind her. Her image appeared in the mirror, showing her sitting in a chair against the far wall. Instead of her normal dress of skirt, boots and leather straps around her breasts, she wore the same business suit in dark blue as before. Lisa didn't turn to her.

"Is this what killing people does to me?" she asked. "I look like I'm over sixty."

"It's how you will look in just a few years," said Vanth. "The mission is draining the life from you."

The effects of the three ornaments prevented Lisa from any sense of dismay. She could only think of the desperate need to kill again.

"How can I continue the mission if there are no Tarquinia to kill?" she asked.

"There are many Tarquinia, but they are not in this country. You must find a way to travel to regions where most of the family emigrated when they were ordered out of Etruria by the Romans."

"That can take months. And I will be too obvious to any law enforcement bodies that look into the deaths."

"I have a way," said Vanth. "Soon, you will return to the mission."

The image vanished. Lisa continued to stare at the image of the old woman in the mirror, feeling only a slight sickness in her stomach at the prospect of looking like that when was perhaps thirty. Finally, she returned the ornaments to the safe and thought about finding a nest of Tarquinia that would let her kill several of them in one session. She felt a lot better after that.

A week later, an advertisement appeared in the local paper, advising that the retirement of one of the town councillors had opened up a vacancy. A special election would be run in a month's time, and applicants should register with the council as intending to run.

"What the hell do I know about being a local government person?" demanded Lisa in some irritation when Vanth appeared in her bedroom. "Or how to run an electoral campaign?"

"I'll see to it," said Vanth. "I will organise leaflets in every letter box, posters around the town, my image will call on every home in the region and arrange glowing biographies in the newspapers."

"But why?" demanded Lisa in irritation. "How is that going to help me locate Tarquinia?"

"You will see," said the Angel of Death and vanished.

*   *   *

"I am delighted to welcome our new Councillor, Lisa Kendricks," said the mayor. "Lisa ran a superb campaign and won by one of the biggest margins on record."

The applause ran round the council chamber. Lisa managed to smile, despite her discomfort with the unfamiliarity of this situation. She felt intense irritation with the Angel of Death for having told her to apply for the position without any explanation of how it would facilitate her mission of killing Tarquinia. She tuned back to the mayor speaking his introduction.

"As you know, Lisa is the daughter of Professor Robert Kendricks, known as one of the world's leading experts on the Etruscan civilisation and head of the department of archaeology at the university until his untimely death several years ago. Please make Lisa welcome and offer all the help you can in making her familiar with our systems and our staff."

Murmurs of approval ran round the conference table before the mayor took control again. "You all have the agenda in front of you, so let's begin. First item, pothole repairs along Market Street..."

The next hour was taken up with items of which Lisa knew very little, but she spent the time watching the byplay between the other councillors, identifying the allies and the enemies and the level of influence each of them appeared to have. Finally, she saw why Vanth had engineered her election.

"May I raise a topic that has never come up before?" said a middle-aged man in a dark suit with a bright yellow tie.

"Of course, Councillor Jamieson," said the mayor. "That sounds interesting."

Jamieson smiled. "We are all increasingly aware and worried about the effects of climate change on the world's weather," he said. "Something that has not yet affected the United Kingdom is a Tsunami, when a tidal wave of extreme size hits a coastal area and wipes out terrible numbers of homes, buildings, infrastructure, taking many lives with it. They result usually from earthquakes in the ocean and travel at extraordinary speeds."

"Your point, Councillor?" said the mayor.

"My point, Mr Mayor, is that while such a catastrophe has not yet hit this country, the likelihood is increasing, according to experts in this field. It must be time to plan ahead for such an event. We are not far from the coast and according to those same experts, could be affected by a Tsunami hitting our coastal region."

"I see your point," said the mayor. "What do you suggest?"

"I have learnt that several small towns on the coast of southern France have already implemented plans for such an event. They combined consultants in a single project and developed detailed plans for warnings, road use, and everything involved in minimising the loss of life. I recommend that we send one of us to that region to see exactly what has been done and then develop the plans for us to do the same."

With a sharp intake of breath, Lisa finally understood why she was here.

"That certainly sounds logical," said the mayor. "The problem is that our budget has been drained by the recent damage to our roads and several buildings in the last big storm and the recent expansion of some of our services. I really don't see how we can afford this."

Lisa saw her moment. She stood up.

"Mr Mayor, Councillors, I believe I can help. I fully endorse Councillor Jamieson's view, this is something we should do urgently. Someone needs to go and see just what these coastal towns have planned. When my parents died, I was left a sizeable inheritance. I would be more than happy to undertake this project and finance it myself."

Two weeks later, Lisa was on a flight to Nice.

Chapter 31 – Tarquinia Hunting

Lisa stepped outside her hotel early in the morning and stopped, shaken. Tarquinia! She could sense the distinctive smell of the family in her ultra-sensitised nostrils. Never before had she sensed such a gathering of the family. She was only a few miles from the Italian border, and it was no surprise that many members of the Etruscan Twelve Families had fled this way when evicted by the Romans, nor a surprise that many had settled just a short distance into a different country.

The wave of Tarquinia scent mixed with the salty sea air from the ocean visible just a block from where she stood. Lisa shivered from a mix of the cool sea air and the anticipation of what would happen in the next few days.

She started walking towards the small town centre. Only a kilometre along the way, she came to the local school and stopped. There were Tarquinian kids in there! She could sense them, energetic and active, a different feel to that of adults. It gave her an idea, though she would need more information before she could develop a plan. She continued walking, excitement building in her.

At the library entrance, another shock hit her. The large, casually dressed man leaving the library with two books under his arm was Tarquinian, she knew immediately. She tried not to stare but couldn't help focusing on his neck where a thrust of a knife would do the job required. She continued into the building. It had the air of all libraries, quiet, a sense of concentration, a few people sitting motionless at tables, reading books. She counted three librarians and eleven readers. One of the librarians, an attractive young woman in her twenties was Tarquinian. Two of the people reading books were the same. So far, Lisa had never encountered more than one Tarquinian at a time. This situation was overwhelming, a feast for her insatiable urge to kill members of the family. Almost trembling, she turned and left, not wishing to be noticed and perhaps remembered at a later time.

She walked on through the centre of the small town and then returned to her hotel. In that short time, she detected two more Tarquinia, an elderly woman in stylish clothing, and a young man in standard jeans and golf-shirt walking a German Shepherd dog.

Back in her room, she sat deep in thought, planning how best to take advantage of the incredible situation in which she had found herself. But the more she pondered the situation, the more the hurdles to overcome appeared. She was a tourist, staying in a hotel in a small town. She had hardly blended into the background, even more a problem being a young, attractive woman. Enough people had already seen her and would remember her. She didn't have a weapon, and she could not kill in her usual way, with a knife and then be able to throw her blood-stained clothing into an incinerator. Nor could she acquire the protective clothing she had worn in the past, the head-to-toe coveralls without causing comment at the store. Nor could she make the cloth coverings for her feet.

An idea came to her. It had a superb advantage, that if it worked, she could kill several Tarquinia at the same time. The fact that it might kill several others who were not Tarquinia didn't disturb her at all. She spent an hour merely savouring the sensation of killing perhaps ten or more Tarquinia in one single move. It tasted exquisite to her.

She went back to the ground floor and took out the small hire car she had rented at the airport on her arrival at Nice airport. She drove to within a kilometre of the school she had seen earlier and parked where she could observe the main entry. The school looked quiet, but she assumed classes were still in progress and would end sometime soon as the school day ended.

She was correct. Only twenty minutes later, a series of bells rang, audible even to Lisa sitting in her car. Minutes later, the first pupils exited from the building, just as a single-decker bus arrived and stopped by the gate. Lisa had expected that. What she had seen was a school big enough for perhaps a hundred students, far more than could live in this small town. So, many more would be sent in from other small towns in the region and some form of public transport would be used to take them back and forth.

A line of children walked out of the gate and entered the bus. Even from this position, Lisa could scent the Tarquinia among that group of more than thirty students.

The bus was soon full and set off along the main road to the next town. Lisa started her car and followed it. The coastal road to the nearest town was winding and followed along a cliff for much of the way. Just a few kilometres out of town, Lisa saw the perfect spot. The road turned sharply left alongside the vertical cliff down to the rocks by the sea. The bus had to slow down significantly to navigate the bend.

All the time Lisa had been following the bus, she had seen only one car coming in the other direction. She stopped the car and sat deep in thought. She had her plan.

* * *

The following morning, Lisa dressed in simple and unremarkable jeans and sweater, took her rental car onto the road. After a short distance, she donned the dark brown wig that she carried with her for just this sort of purpose and went into town. The hardware store looked remarkably like the hardware store at home and looked well populated as she drove past and parked a kilometre away before walking back.

She found the boxcutter quickly, paid for it in Euros without speaking to the cashier and left to return to her hotel, removing the wig before she reached it. She was sure nobody could connect her to the woman who had made the purchase in the hardware store.

Shortly before the school day ended, she drove back to where she had watched before, saw the bus stop by the front gate and counted thirty-two children climb aboard. As before, she sensed several Tarquinia in that line. She started up the car, drove past the bus and well ahead to the point she had identified before, about fifty metres before the steep drop to the rocks below. She stopped by the side of the road, donned the wig again, though this time she was dressed in a grey track suit. She slipped on the thin gloves she had bought in England before leaving.

She saw the bus in her rear-view mirror and got out of the car. As the bus approached, she waved it down, putting on an expression of huge distress. As expected, the bus slowed and stopped, the road-side door opened, and the male driver spoke to her. She couldn't understand the rapid French but pointed back at the car. The driver smiled, waved her aboard.

She had rehearsed the next moves in her mind all day. She climbed up the steps, holding the boxcutter, thumbed open the blade and bent over the startled driver. A single slice cut his throat wide open. She bent a little further, clicked open the seat belt round his lap, hauled him out of his seat and flung him to the road through the open door. Ignoring the screams from the children, she slid quickly into the driver's seat, engaged the gear and turned the wheel towards the edge of the road. Smoothly, she slid out of the seat and leaped out of the open door, running back towards her car. The bus continued moving, reached the edge of the road, covered the short distance of rough ground and smashed through the simple wooden fence that served as a warning, rather than a safety barrier. It fell down the cliff and smashed into the rocks.

Lisa watched it in great satisfaction, feeling the warm glow of exhilaration, she had felt before when she killed a Tarquinian. The deaths of perhaps another twenty innocent children didn't affect her at all. But the multiple deaths of Tarquinia tasted even sweeter than she had anticipated.

She walked back to her car and returned to the hotel. She had stripped off the blood-covered gloves and put them in a plastic bag she had brought. She boiled water in a pan on the tiny kitchen facilities her room contained and placed the boxcutter in it, leaving it for a few minutes which she was certain would have cleaned away any possible trace of blood. Later, she scrubbed the pan carefully to remove any further remaining traces. She had seen enough cop shows to have some idea of just how brilliant the current level of forensic technology was, but she was certain she had left nothing that could be identified as blood on the boxcutter and the pan.

She unwrapped the plastic bag containing the bloodied gloves and deposited them in the bathroom sink, soaking in water for an hour. After that, she rinsed them out and returned them to the sink covered in vinegar. She was sure that would destroy any possible

DNA she had left on the inside surface. Later, she intended to wrap them in a second bag and deposit them in a garbage bin in town. The first bag, with blood traces, she burned in the kitchen sink and washed the remains down the drain.

She was certain she had left nothing that could tie her to the killing of thirty-two children. She had killed several Tarquinia and that was cause for enormous satisfaction.

Less than half an hour later, she heard multiple police sirens racing past the hotel. She walked downstairs and saw a line of cars and several ambulances racing at dangerous speeds out in the direction of where she had been. The sidewalks were crowded with people. Walking inside, she saw the hotel manager in intense conversation with others. She knew he spoke good English.

"What is going on?" she asked him. She could see the distress in his face.

"There has been an accident," the man said. "We don't know all the details, only that the school bus went over the cliff and down to the rocks. We have no idea of how the children are."

"Oh my God," explained Lisa. "That's dreadful."

She returned to her room to think about her next steps. Quickly, she realised that her first impulse, to leave and return home was wrong. Once the body of the driver had been found, his throat cut, the police would realise that this was a murder. They would interrogate almost everybody in the region and foreigners staying in a hotel would be the first suspects. If she left, that would set the hounds on the chase, and they would trace her rapidly. She would have to stay.

That evening, she tuned her little radio into an English language station and listened carefully. It didn't take long to hear what she was waiting for.

"News has reached us of an appalling mass murder in the south of France," said the well-educated tones of the newsreader. "A bus carrying thirty-two children aged between seven and eleven went over a cliff just a few kilometres from their school, while it was returning the children to their home town a short distance away. The bus crashed into rocks over fifty metres down and all the children were killed. This has been declared a multiple homicide because the body of the driver was found by the side of the road where the bus went off. He had been murdered. The police are not releasing any further details of this death. The whole region is in deep shock and grief. The French President has declared a day of mourning. The police are conducting an intensive investigation."

Lisa felt a strong surge of satisfaction. This had been the first multiple killing of Tarquinia and it exhilarated her. The deaths of so many innocent children didn't bother her at all. She considered it merely collateral damage, a bonus payment to the Etruscan Angel of Death.

* * *

It was no surprise that the hotel owner told the five residents that he could not provide the normal service but also recognised that they could not leave until the police had talked to them. But he made the kitchen available, and said they could use it as they wished.

The police came the following day. Lisa was the third to be interviewed and she sat in the lounge with the detective.

"I don't speak French," she said on sitting down.

"Not a problem," replied the detective. He was elderly, dressed in a smart suit and wore horn-rimmed glasses. "Now, Miss Kendricks, why are you in this area?" He displayed not a trace of any accent. He could have been a well-educated, British detective.

Lisa explained the assignment she was on for her local council. She took out the letter of introduction the council had prepared for her to show to the local body, and the notes she had written already, based on what she had been told by the local people and the signposting the council had erected for local people to get away as easily as possible if the Tsunami sirens went off.

"You appear to have driven around the region quite extensively," said the detective as he studied the documents. "You have registered on the traffic cameras several times."

"I was looking at all the escape routes that the council here had signposted in the event of a Tsunami.

You can see the pictures I have taken of those, as well as the notes from the local council."

The detective nodded. He seemed quite satisfied and stood up, handing back the notes Lisa had given him.

"Please remain here for three more days in case we have to talk again," he said.

That suited Lisa well. She planned to move around the town and see the grief that her actions had caused. She knew it would give her great satisfaction and emphasise the euphoria she was feeling from the multiple deaths.

She followed that plan and was highly gratified to see the huge distress in the town. Almost everywhere she went, the sounds of weeping could be heard in shops and houses and in the library. When she saw more people she recognised as Tarquinia, she still felt the urge to kill, but it was somewhat sated by the more than thirty children she had killed. Perhaps she could come back another time and attend to the business that was on offer here.

Three days later, she returned to England, well satisfied by the results. Her calendar echoed the sensation of extra girth and weight. She was three months pregnant, and she knew that her lifestyle had to change for a while. As she sat in her lounge, one day, she sensed the arrival of the demonic presence.

"What am I going to do?" she asked when the demon Angel of Death appeared. The demon had donned conventional clothing, not her usual warlike attire.

"You must take no risks," said the woman in her long blue dress, seated in the armchair across from Lisa. "This coming child is critical to our plans. You cannot spend time in prison, and you must not engage in any more killings for now. Your physical abilities are limited, a potential victim might reverse the situation. This must not happen."

"But I still have the need to kill. Sometimes it is almost overwhelming. How can I last more than six months without satisfying it?"

"I can reduce that need," said the woman. "We in the Underworld will also feel the lack of new deaths, but this can be withstood. The long-term plans depend on your child."

"Why?" demanded Lisa, feeling huge distress. "What is she going to be?"

"That is not for you to know."

"I'm not going to keep her. I can't manage being a mother with a child and probably having to travel to find Tarquinia to kill."

The woman opposite nodded.

"That is logical. We will find suitable adoptive parents and have them eager to take the child."

"What does 'suitable' mean?"

"This is not necessary for you to know."

The woman vanished.

Lisa's nightmares began that night.

"What has happened to you?" The voice was of Lisa's young self, it had a pleading, distressed quality. "How could you possibly have become so insane that you can kill more than thirty children and not feel a thing?"

Even in her dream, Lisa felt massive distress. On a few occasions, she had asked herself the same question, knowing that underneath the satisfaction of having killed several Tarquinia, she also wondered at the lack of any emotion at the deaths of so many innocent children who had died, simply because they were on the same bus as her intended victims.

"I can't help it," she pleaded. "I'm cursed, it's too strong for me to stop doing what I do."

"You have to," said the little voice. "This child growing inside you, she's evil. She's carrying the same curse. They will take you to Hell when you die, but your child will continue to kill innocents."

Lisa woke up weeping heavily, a sense of utter doom enveloping her.

Much the same happened the next night.

"Don't you remember how you were when you were eight or nine?" said the little voice from the depths of a disturbed dream. "You played with dolls, you had friends, you weren't this pathological serial killer. Haven't you thought that this whole thing is in your mind, there is no curse, you've made it all up to justify the need to kill?"

Even in her dream, this shook Lisa. The idea that she had created the whole story of a curse, imagined the demonic visits, was it all to justify the terrible killing lust?

"You need help," continued her younger self. "Go to a psychiatrist."

"How can I?" Even in her dream, she knew how impossible that was. "As soon as I talk about the people I have killed, a doctor would hand me over to the police."

Lisa woke up gasping for air. She realised she had stopped breathing for a time. She sat upright, breathing deeply, trying to calm down, remembering the conversation that had taken place.

A psychiatrist was out of the question, she knew. However psychopathic she had become, going for professional help would mean the end of any life outside of a prison.

"Then an exorcist," said her younger self. "And get an abortion, like you did last time. This new one is worse than you, she will carry on killing innocents."

Lisa began to feel torn apart. Her subconscious mind had suggested an exorcism. But how could that be any different from a psychiatrist? Lisa had never practiced any religion, but she had the idea that a priest could not reveal the details of a confession. But a confession of so many killings? Could a priest not inform the law? She knew she could never risk it.

Lisa did not sleep again that night.

Chapter 32 – The Hounds Return

"Funny how we keep returning to this bloody case," said Detective Inspector James Brigham, still radiating pride at his recent promotion.

"And bloody frustrating that we never cracked it," agreed Detective Chief Inspector Adrian Cooper. "Christ, you were a Sergeant when we first got it, and Mary was just a Constable."

"Senior Constable, please Guv," said Detective Sergeant Mary Stanton, hiding her smile. "Anyway, we did crack it, we got Lisa Kendricks dead to rights, she should still be in her lifetime sentence without parole, but that very strange attorney somehow got her off. Did we ever find out who he was?"

"Something very fishy about that bloke," said Brigham. "We never did trace him. I still can't understand why we didn't prosecute her. Something weird happened. I reckon that bloke messed with our minds. Why didn't we refer her to the Crown Prosecutor?"

"And that was, what, ten years ago?" commented Cooper. "And here we are again, because Mary called the meeting. Okay, Mary, what's on your mind?"

The Senior Sergeant arranged some documents on her lap.

"Guv, as you know, I asked for permission to keep tracking the movements of Lisa Kendricks, and you and the Chief Superintendent were happy to give it to me because we all were convinced that she was as guilty as hell for a number of murders."

"Damn right," muttered Brigham.

"What he said," added Cooper with a small grin.

Mary ignored them.

"As part of my project, I contacted Interpol offices in Europe and asked to be kept up to date with murders of a particular type anywhere in Europe. All the ones for which we liked Lisa were stabbing deaths, that seems to be her chief Modus Operandi, so that's what I asked Interpol to tell me about."

"Sensible," said Cooper. "Otherwise you'd be swamped with communications."

Mary grimaced. "Hell, I was swamped already. Bloody amazing how many people get stabbed in Europe every week. Anyway, being a modern lady cop, I talked to the computer gurus down at the Met and asked for help. They started yapping about Artificial Intelligence, which sounded cool, and they were certainly enthusiastic about the possibilities when I started telling them about some of the weird features of the deaths we had already identified."

"What, all that stuff about many of the dead 'uns had Northern Italy in their DNA?"

"That indeed," replied Mary. "Also, the very strange fact that after a number of these deaths, there were two others at almost the same minute that occurred within two or three days of the murder, but without any identifiable cause. And those displayed Northern Italy in their DNA."

"What all of them?" Cooper looked sceptical.

"No, Guv, as it turned out, not all the dead 'uns as you so poetically put it, had that Italian ancestry, but many of them did. But all the ones who died inexplicably immediately after, they all showed Northern Italy markers in their DNA."

"Well, shit, eh?" said Cooper. "So how has this project worked out?"

"What I asked these techie gurus to do was set up a model which would relate any postmortems of stabbing deaths that showed the Italian marker, to any incidents of deaths without obvious cause that occurred almost at the same time and within three days of the stabbing murder, and indicate also if the Italian marker showed up in the DNA."

"Hell's bloody bells," said Brigham. "You couldn't do that manually. That Artificial Intelligence thing might have some uses, after all. What did you come up with?"

"They did list three such cases, so then I tracked Lisa's movements at the time those murders were committed, and surprise, surprise, she was within an hour's drive each time. But then I changed the parameters just a couple of days ago, when the news came of that horrible tragedy in Southern France when over thirty kids died when a bus went over the cliff."

"Why that one?" asked Cooper. "Nobody got stabbed."

"No, Guv, but get this. Lisa Kendricks was in the town near where it happened. All those kids were at a school in that town, and they were on a school bus taking them home at the end of the day."

"WHAT?" Both men exploded with the same exclamation.

"Yes," said Mary. "She'd arrived a few days earlier, ostensibly on an assignment for the local council to which she'd been elected recently. So I asked the guys to expand the model to look at any form of death in just the last ten days."

"Christ on a crutch, Mary, did your techie guys come up with anything?"

"They did, Guv. Would you two guys get hold of your underpants, because the postmortems revealed that twelve of the dead kids had Northern Italy markers in their DNA. Eight of them from one family grouping, four from another. And then data came in showing that six people died without cause, all within seconds of each other in France, Germany and Greece. All of them had the same DNA marker as the four kids. I'm still expecting to hear of more sudden deaths over the next few days. It seems like those sudden deaths occurred in pairs, two deaths very soon after each stabbing death. I'll lay odds that if we got all the information, we'd hear about a total of sixteen sudden deaths, all within minutes or hours of the eight kids with the same family grouping.”

“This is just insane,” said Cooper with some force. “It makes no sense at all.”

“Something else to add to the insanity,” said Mary. Her calm exterior was not matched by the tears that ran slowly down her cheeks. “I’ve asked for DNA results of all the stabbings that occurred in Europe. Quite a few had that same DNA marker as the eight kids in the bus, but even more weird, every single one of the associated deaths without explanation had the same DNA marker as the four kids in the crash.”

“This is not humanly possible,” said Brigham, huge distress showing in his face and body. “What you’re saying is that the killer, probably Lisa Kendricks had killed a number of people, but the ones with Northern Italian ancestry all had the markers of one family group, while all the sudden deaths apparently associated with those murders, all had the markers of the other family group.”

“That seems to be the case,” said Mary.

At that moment, Brigham dropped dead in his seat.

* * *

“Never a single warning about his health,” said Cooper. “He’s had the regular medicals that we all have, not a mention in his reports of any problem. And still no indication of why he died. The pathologist is utterly baffled. This has never happened to him before.”

He and Mary Stanton sat in the Chief Inspector's office, seeking some mutual support in the pain of the shock of their colleague's sudden death.

"We've worked together for thirteen years," said Mary. "He was my mentor when I joined the force, and we covered more cases than I can remember. But he never showed anything worse than a cold one winter."

"I was a sergeant when I met him the first time," said Cooper. He played idly with his pen, twirling it around, his eyes not lifting from the desktop. "I knew then we had a bloke with talent. God, I'm going to miss him."

The knock on the door broke the pain-filled atmosphere. A policewoman entered and handed Cooper a single sheet of paper. Cooper acknowledged it with a wave and she left.

"His DNA examination," he said. "All normal, nothing to raise concerns, British birth to a long line of British people from mainly Sussex, and.." He paused, his jaw dropping in shock. "Ancestry goes back to Northern Italy, in that second family group, the ones that died without cause within a day or two after the death of somebody in the first group."

He and Mary stared at each other, the impossible fact making them both almost catatonic.

"Oh my God," said Mary. "What the hell is going on?"

Chapter 33 – A New Generation

The next day, Lisa got up soon after five, unable to get any rest at all. But she had an odd sense of something having changed in her. She forced down a breakfast of toast and coffee, struggling to identify what had happened. Only later in the morning, did she realise what it was. The lust to kill, something that was always in her head, though strongest when she thought of the Tarquinia family, was almost non-existent. She could sense tiny traces of it, but the power was negligible.

Curious, she went to her safe and extracted the three ornaments, sat before her dressing table mirror and put them on. Nothing happened. Instead of the usual rush of warmth, power and a surge of killing needs, she seemed unchanged.

"I told you I would reduce it until you have had your child," said the voice of the demon.

Lisa looked behind her but saw nothing. She remembered the demon telling her that but felt no comfort from the effect.

"I don't want to have this child," she said, the first thing that came to her mind.

"You have no choice in the matter."

"What if I have another abortion?"

"If you make that decision, I will cause you such pain that you will beg for relief," said the demon. "You *will* have this child."

"But in all this, what is there for me? An early death, descent into your Etruscan Hell? At least that would stop the killing and if I don't have the child, there would be nobody to carry on your curse. Killing myself now would be a better solution for the world." Even with the fear of the path to Hell, Lisa saw a way out of the continual killing.

"Yes, that is a way out," said the voice of Lisa the child. "You may be damned, but many people would not die before their time."

"You must not do that," exclaimed the demon. Even in this stressed situation, Lisa heard the alarm in the voice of the Angel of Death. "If you do, or even try, your time in Hell will be a hundred times worse. I cannot tell you the agonies you will endure for twice as long as the regular sentence."

Lis shivered and felt panic wash over her like a tidal wave. She shivered, took off the ornaments and replaced them in the safe. She knew she was trapped. She could end the killing, but at the price of her immediate death and two thousand years of agony in the Etruscan Hell. Or she could follow the path set for her by the curse of more than twenty-five hundred years ago and know that many more innocent people would die at the hands of her and her future daughter.

Lisa fell to the floor, sobbing uncontrollably.

Two more nights of stressed nightmares, listening to her younger self beg her to take a path that would end the Earthly nightmare, if not her own damnation, Lisa was a wreck. She was afraid to look in the mirror, because now she saw the images that she had seen before, where her reflection was of a much older woman, her face badly lined, drawn and unhealthy. She barely ate, usually vomiting when she tried, and her weight declined badly. To her horror, the beautiful young girl she had been had become an ugly old woman.

On the third day, as she sat frozen in her lounge, there was knock on the door. Startled, she looked up, unable to move immediately. The knock was repeated. This time, Lisa stood up, sensing an extraordinary presence. She walked to the door.

"Who's there?" she demanded.

"My name used to be Larce," said a young man's voice.

"Used to be? What does that mean?"

"That was my name when the curse was placed on the Tarquinia."

Lisa was stunned. How could anyone know about this? Trembling, she opened the door to see a man of perhaps thirty years old, dressed in slacks, a blue blazer and a white shirt. He could have been a prosperous executive on his way to play golf.

Shaking inside, she stared at him. He looked innocent enough, but the power radiating from him was palpable.

"I think you need my help," the man said.

Still shaking, finding it difficult to stand, she opened the door further and stood aside. He walked through and went directly to the lounge, sitting down in the armchair last occupied by the Angel of Death. Lisa took the opposite seat, hardly able to breath and trembling hard.

"My name was Larce when the curse was laid by the Vulci against the Tarquinia," said the newcomer.

Lisa shook her head in confusion. "What are these names? Tarquinia? Vulci? What are you talking about?

"They were two of the Twelve Families that ruled the Etruscan tribes for several thousand years. They had lived in enmity for hundreds of years and each of them laid a curse on the other."

"A curse? Is this what has caused my damnation?"

Deep inside her mind, Lisa somehow knew that she had once known these facts, but had somehow had her mind cleared of the memories. Was this the work of the Angel of Death?

"Yes, Lisa, it is."

"That was over twenty-five hundred years ago. How can you be from that time?"

"This body is borrowed. The owner will regain it when we are done, and he will have no memory of the events."

Somehow, Lisa believed him. "Are you the priest that laid the curse?"

"No, that was my brother, Charun. Once, he had been a priest of the True Gods, as was I, but he embraced the Gods of the Underworld. Now he is still paying for it in that Underworld, though his time is nearly done."

Lisa's head was spinning in confusion. She was talking to a young man who somehow held the presence of a priest from over two thousand years ago, telling her about a curse laid between two ancient families. She felt slightly sick at the thought and struggled to see anything rational in what was happening.

"You said you could help me?" Lisa felt a surge of hope, sensing the truth in what the man had told her, despite the impossibility of it. "How did you know that I needed it?"

The man smiled. "The younger version of you called out. She is in huge distress, and I heard it."

"And will you be able to help me at all?"

"It is not certain. That was a powerful curse, laid by the most powerful of the priests of the Underworld. But I can ask the True Gods for their help and perhaps reduce the hold it has on you."

"If there's a chance, I beg you to take it." Lisa felt a trickle of hope run through her.

The man stood up, closed his eyes and seemed to concentrate for several minutes, while Lisa sat quietly, occasional tremors still running through her. Suddenly the man moved and began walking clockwise round Lisa's seat, emitting a soft tone in a tenor drone that ranged up and down a pair of octaves. He stopped, faced Lisa and started speaking. The words were quite unintelligible to her, but there was a cadence, a rhythm that was pleasing.

He stopped. Again, he stood still for several minutes, his eyes closed.

"That may do it," he said. "But I cannot guarantee it. I have appealed to the True Gods for sympathy for you, to lift the curse and save you from further unpleasantness. I got only an acknowledgement of my plea, but no indication of what the result will be."

Lisa found herself weeping hard, hiding her face in her hands.

"I hope that's true," said the voice of the younger Lisa.

When Lisa lifted her face again, the man had gone.

* * *

Six months went by, and Lisa took herself to the hospital as she sensed the imminent arrival of her daughter. In that time, she had filed papers to have the child adopted immediately upon birth and had heard that a family in Birmingham had applied to take her and been approved. Lisa felt nothing on hearing that news.

"Do you want the painkiller?" asked the elderly nurse in the hospital ward.

"Yes please," replied Lisa, but added nothing more.

Over the next six hours, she experienced increasing contractions, signs that the baby was about to arrive, and when the doctor ordered her moved to the birthing room, she was happy to receive the spinal injection that made her barely conscious for the next two hours. When she regained some awareness, a nurse was standing before her.

"You have a very healthy baby girl," said the nurse with a broad smile. "Congratulations. Would you like to see her?"

Lisa shook her head. "Have her adoptive parents arrived?"

"They've been here the whole time you were having her. They'd like to see you."

"No," said Lisa. "She's being adopted. Better if I know nothing about it."

"Okay," said the nurse, not able to hide her surprise, and she left the ward.

When a new face in a white coat entered the ward, Lisa spoke first.

"I suppose you're the psychiatrist coming to see what's wrong with me?"

The psychiatrist smiled. "Yes I am. I'm curious as to why you have refused either to see your child or to meet the adoptive parents. It's most unusual."

"Why should I want to see either? They represent a time of my life I want to forget."

"What about the child's father? Shouldn't he have a say in this?"

"Maybe, if I knew who the father was. I fucked several guys around that time. I've no idea which one is the father, and I don't care. They were all lousy in bed, anyway."

There was not a lot in the doctor's experience that dismayed him, but this did.

"I don't think I can help you, Lisa. I wish you well."

"You can fuck off as well," she said to the retreating back.

Lisa recovered rapidly over the next two days and went home. She had felt nothing about having had a child and letting it go without seeing it. She didn't even look at the paperwork she had been given to learn the name and location of the adopting family and felt no curiosity about the name the child had been given.

Chapter 34 – A Crisis

Lisa spent a month doing little but watching television and reading magazines. Sometimes, she worried that being this inactive could not be healthy, but she excused herself by claiming that she needed to recover from the birth. At no time did she feel any regret or sadness at having let the child be taken away without even seeing her.

At other times, she sensed relief that the intervention of the Etruscan priest, Larce, in the body of the young man whose name she never asked, had apparently worked. She felt no urge to kill, though she still feared the possibility of the Etruscan Hell when she died. But the exorcism appeared to have been successful.

She was wrong.

After six weeks, she began to feel irritation frequently erupting in her thoughts. At first, she couldn't identify the cause, but after two more weeks, it burst into her head like an exploding firework.

She needed to kill again.

The realisation was terrifying. The priest had failed. She spent hours sitting in the dark, trying to call on the priest to come to her again, but nothing worked. Then one evening, she took the ornaments from her safe, sat before the dressing table mirror and slowly donned all three.

The results were as they had always been. Her body flushed with the deep urge to kill, especially Tarquinia, though at first, she knew that any killing would do. In the mirror, the image of Lisa slowly changed from her present appearance of a woman in her thirties, to that of someone much older. It dismayed Lisa to see this change. The woman in the mirror looked aged and unhealthy, her skin a sallow colour, almost yellow in places. Bags under her eyes had become larger and her mouth had changed from what had been a pleasant shape to one of thin lips and down-turned corners in an expression of permanent disapproval. *Was this how she would look in just a few more years, aged far beyond her time?* she wondered in distress.

"Did you seriously think you could escape the curse?"

The image of Vanth, the Angel of Death appeared in the mirror. She was dressed as she appeared in many Etruscan images, a short skirt, knee-high boots, her breasts covered with several leather straps round her torso. The face was ugly, no humour, no warmth to be seen.

Lisa gasped as if in pain.

"I thought I could," she rasped, tension constricting her throat.

"But you don't want to anymore, do you?" said Vanth, her tones mocking. "That meddling fool, Larce, actually thought he could cleanse you. He couldn't, the Gods ignored his silly prancing and howling."

Lisa couldn't reply.

"But you do want to escape it," begged the voice the

child Lisa, somewhere in her head. "Please, Lisa, tell her, this is just too terrible, it's not what we were when we were young, tell her we want out of this."

Vanth laughed. "You think that silly infant can tell me to lift the curse? Listen, you little fool, I can no more lift that curse than I can fly to the Moon. Only the old Gods can do that, and they don't seem willing, and I have no wish to ask them."

The child in Lisa's mind did not respond, whether out of shock or because the truth of the Demon's statement was obvious, Lisa could not explain herself. The power of the ornaments was so strong and seemed to be growing. Lisa had no further doubts about what she wanted to do.

"Where do I find Tarquinia?" she asked. "There are none here."

"You must go back to the region where you found your previous plentiful prey. That region of France was where many Etruscans fled when the Romans forced them out. It will be good hunting for you again."

The image vanished. Lisa removed the ornaments, her mind filled with two main thoughts, exhilaration at knowing where her next victims were and some frustration at wondering how to kill them without drawing attention to herself. As she pulled out the atlas from her shelves and began locating the best place to go for her next bout of Tarquinia killing, the child's voice broke into her mind again.

"Lisa, please don't go," she said. "You don't have to do this."

"Yes I do," said Lisa aloud. "You heard what Vanth said, I have no choice. I'm cursed with having to kill Tarquinia, I have no option. I'm going to Hell, anyway."

"You don't know that," said the child. "Maybe that Priest, Larce asked the Gods to ease that punishment, he told you that, maybe they heard him. Please, Lisa, stop doing this."

Lisa began to weep. "I have no choice. I'm damned. Stop whining at me."

"Not until you agree not to keep doing this. You can be saved."

"Shut up!" shouted Lisa.

To her dismay, the Angel of Death, Vanth appeared again.

"That child needs killing." Vanth was still dressed in the traditional garb shown in most of the illustrations of her. "I'll see what I can do. Meanwhile Lisa, don't stop planning your trip. You need to kill more Tarquinia and soon. That is your mission and if you fail to follow it, I will inflict great pain on you until you commit to it."

"I think not," said a man's voice. Startled, Lisa stared at the new arrival. He was tall, dressed in robes of an ancient age and he stood facing Vanth, staring down at her.

"Larce, how dare you?" shouted Vanth. "How dare you face me, the Angel of Death and defy my words? Be gone, before I personally take you to Hell to face eons of torments."

Lisa was trembling. *What the hell was going on?* She was in a room with one of the ancient Gods of Etruria and the priest of over two thousand years ago who had tried to help her before but now looked as he had in his own time. Something was going on, so far above her head that terror nearly enveloped her. She could only watch a titanic battle of wills take place.

"I am here because the True Gods have sent me," said Larce. His voice was clear and strong. He showed no fear of the Angel of Death and her threats.

"Your gods are dead," sneered Vanth. "There are only the gods of the Underworld left, and they will embrace you soon to show you what happens to those who defy us."

"Let me show you how false are your words," said Larce. He didn't move, but the scene changed in ways that were incomprehensible and terrifying to Lisa.

The room was vast, like a ballroom, but bleak and gloomy. There was no furniture, except for a large chair on a slight platform at one end. Seated in that chair was a man who radiated power and authority. He seemed immense, and to either side of him, stood a figure bathed in light. To Lisa, she could only think of them as Angels. Vanth, the Angel of Death stood alone, a few metres away from the seated man. Lisa found herself about the same distance away, and just two metres from Vanth.

"We are in the Etruscan Hell," said a voice behind. Lisa turned to see Larce. But even more astonishing, next to him stood a woman that Lisa recognised. It was the detective, Mary Stanton. She looked frozen in fear, her hands over her mouth and the trembles could almost be felt radiating from her.

"Do not fear, Mary," said Larce. His voice was soothing and his face kindly as he touched the detective on her shoulder. "I have brought you here because you are so close to realising what is going on in your world and I want you to see what will happen next." He turned back to Lisa.

"My plea to the gods didn't go unnoticed, Lisa. Even though your need to kill rose in you again, the True Gods heard me and have considered my plea." He stopped and turned to face the entity on the small platform.

"We of the Rasenna Gods thought we had been left to live in peace," said the man. His voice filled every corner of the huge room. It was powerful and Lisa felt the energy from it sink into every atom of her body. Strangely, it calmed her completely and a sideways glance at Mary showed that she too, had lost her fear and now stared, fascinated at the speaker and at Vanth, the Angel of Death. Lisa realised that this was an experience that no other modern human had ever been given.

"Larce," said the incredible voice, "you asked that the curse on this woman be lifted, and she not face any time in Hell as a result of her actions."

"I did," said Larce. "The curse was placed by a priest of the Underworld, not a servant of the True Gods. It demanded that just one person, a female of the Vulci Family before maidenhood be cursed with the need to kill anyone in the Tarquinian Family, throughout all of time. The members of both families were dispersed around the world soon after and the hatred and violence of that feud are no longer relevant."

"It was placed by your brother, it seems."

"To my shame, it was."

"And he is still receiving his torments for that crime and others, for far longer than is normally imposed, so great was his crime."

Larce didn't respond and the entity turned its attention to Vanth. As he looked at her, the Demon seemed to shrink a little and her face showed profound fear.

"More than two thousand years later, you have been the main force in keeping this woman in killing mode. Why is that? What value is it to the gods of the Underworld to keep this slaughter continuing?"

"The woman is a natural killer," said Vanth. "We saw that before she was touched by the curse. We didn't choose her to carry on the curse, it was her father who started it with the gift of a gold necklace from the Vulci Family, one of the three items cursed by the Priest,

Charun. When she found the ring without any intervention by us, the path was set, and we saw the way to keep the curse going. It was an obvious move to bring her the copper bracelet. So we did little to restart the curse, we just took the perfect opportunity."

"But why did you need to?" The immense power of the voice held a trace of mockery, Lisa thought. "Was the Underworld running out of victims?"

Vanth seemed also to hear the mockery as she looked defensive. "Our role in this world that you once controlled, was to punish the wrongdoers, the unfaithful. Without those, what reason did we have to maintain the Underworld, once the Rasenna had left it?" She paused for a few moments then spoke again, this time louder, in great anger. "And why are you here to condemn what I do? You and the old Gods, you left us two thousand years ago and went somewhere else. You betrayed the Rasenna. We of the Underworld, we are the only Gods of the Rasenna now, you have no authority here."

The entity sat back in its seat. Lisa realised this was the lord of all the ancient Gods of the Etruscans and she was filled with a sense of wonder.

"We left because there was no need for us," the God said. "But we never thought that the Gods of the Underworld would sanction cruelty and murder and the destruction of the life of a child, as you have done. And our authority? Let me show you my authority."

Vanth screamed in immense pain. She doubled

over and fell to the ground, moaning and spitting blood. And as it started, it stopped. Slowly, Vanth got back to her feet, but the pain showed in the horror reflected in her face.

"The True Gods of the Rasenna left this time and place when our people were dispersed by the Romans," continued the Godlike entity as if nothing had happened. "It is tragic that the Gods of the Underworld felt it necessary to maintain their function. But the True Gods did not place this curse and so we cannot lift it completely. It must remain on the items that the demon cursed."

Lisa felt a jolt of terror at these words. Was she to remain damned for all of time because of this? She realised the God was looking at her.

"But Lisa, I can do this. I can give you the strength to resist the lust to kill if you choose to use it. And I can reduce the time you must spend here when you die. You will not spend a thousand years undergoing the torture that was called for you. You will spend a century without pain, but you will be required to serve the Underworld in ways I cannot forecast."

Lisa still felt too stunned to speak and could only nod.

"Vanth," continued the Old God. "You will cease your efforts to maintain the damnation curse on this woman. You will not approach her again until she dies, and then you can fulfil your real task and escort her to the Underworld where she will remain for only one hundred years."

The scene flickered out of existence and Lisa found herself back in her room.

There was no word from the child in her mind.

* * *

"My god, Guv, you won't believe the crazy dream I had last night." Mary Stanton flopped into the seat across from the desk where Cooper sat, studying some documents.

"What was it?" asked Cooper. He seemed distracted, studying the sheet of paper on his desk.

Mary almost decided not to tell him, but it was so stunning, she just had to.

"All about this damned case about Lisa Kendricks," she said. "It must be getting to me. I dreamed I was taken to some place that was called the Etruscan Hell. Lisa was with me, so were two utter weirdos, some ancient geek in medieval clothing called Larce, apparently. What sort of name is that, anyway? And there was another woman, some ugly old cow in a short skirt and her boobs were all tied up in leather straps. It was all so clear and bloody terrifying."

She stopped and sipped thoughtfully at the mug of coffee she had brought into Cooper's office.

"And then there was some god-like bloke on a throne, it seemed to be some sort of trial. There was something about a Vulci family and a Tarquinian family. God, it was frightening, I don't think I slept a wink after waking up from that."

Cooper looked up from the study of his paper. "What was that about Vulci and Tarquinian?" he asked. There was tension in his voice.

"Those names came up, something about a curse between them. Honest Guv, I was so frightened, the nightmare was so real."

"This paper came an hour ago from the laboratory people," said Cooper. "They've been using the most advanced DNA study techniques, and they've found a lot of stuff. It seems that the area of Northern Italy that so many of the bodies have shown in their DNA, was known as Etruria and a civilisation called Etruscans owned it until about the time of Christ, when they were kicked out by the Romans."

Mary stared at him. "Etruscans? Shit boss, they talked about the Etruscan Hell in my dream."

"And the rest is even weirder, Mary. As we already knew, they'd identified the markers in the DNA as being from two separate groups, but now they've got more accurate. Serious experts in DNA research took samples from the teeth of corpses in those tombs. Apparently, DNA from teeth lasts longer than from anywhere else. Most of the victims of the stabbing attacks came from a tribal group, or family known as Tarquinia. So now they know that all the people who died suddenly without cause, including our colleague, came from a family group known as Vulci. Historians know that they were two of twelve main families that ruled the Etruscans. And the kids on the bus? Four of them were Vulci, eight were Tarquinian."

Mary had her head in her hands. "Jesus Harold Christ, Guv, what the fuck have we got here? And how the hell did I dream all that?"

"That frightens me, Mary. How could you possibly have known about Etruscans? Have you ever heard the name before?"

She sat up and shook her head. "Not that I know of. But I suppose I could have heard it on a television documentary or something. But that doesn't explain how it was in my dream last night, just as we're learning about the civilisation. Guv, I think I may be going out of my mind. And why did I dream Lisa was there?"

"I suppose that's more logical," said Cooper. "We're all sure Lisa was involved in those murders, so she's fairly dominant in your thoughts. But if she was the killer in this story, how did she manage to kill the majority of her victims that were Tarquinian? Not all of them were, but only those that were, then had a couple of Vulci people die soon after. How did Lisa accomplish that, if she really did?"

Mary took several deep breaths.

"I think we have to go and talk to Lisa again."

"I think we do," said Cooper.

Chapter 35 – Some Clarity

The shock that erupted when Lisa opened the door to the two detectives was almost like a small earthquake. Lisa took a step backward, her eyes wide open and she emitted a sharp gasp. Mary Stanton felt a severe jolt run through her body and her gasp of dismay was almost a sob. The two women stared at each other in a silent communication of sheer terror. Cooper almost felt the energy blow up between them and he also felt a tremor of fear. Something incomprehensible was going on, he knew.

Lisa found her voice first.

"What are you doing here, Mary? And why this man? Who is he?"

Mary took a deep breath.

"You know exactly why we're here, Lisa. We'd better come inside."

Lisa stood aside and the two detectives walked in. Cooper showed his warrant card.

"Detective Chief Inspector Adrian Cooper," he said. "I've been working with Detective Senior Sergeant Stanton and Detective Inspector James Brigham ever since those murders of old homeless men more than twenty years ago. We met then."

Lisa barely looked at him. She was still staring at Mary, her face white.

Without being asked, all three took seats in the lounge room. Mary began the proceedings.

"Lisa, a few days ago, a bus crashed in the South of France, killing thirty-two children. You were in the area. Why was that?"

Lisa was obviously struggling for self-control.

"I'm a councillor on the local council," she replied. "We wanted to know about how small coastal towns were preparing for Tsunamis and this town had advanced plans that had received international approval. I went to study them."

"Why you?"

"I volunteered. I'm a rich woman and I offered to cover my own costs to save the council."

Mary threw the bomb.

"Lisa, eight of those children were Tarquinia. Four were Vulci. Was that a factor in your presence? How did you cause that crash?"

Lisa gasped loudly, her hands raised to her mouth, the whites of her eyes obvious.

"How.. why.. How do you know that?" Her voice was barely audible.

"And now we know that the majority of your victims over the last few years were Tarquinia," continued Mary. "And we know that for every Tarquinian you killed, two Vulci people died without any medical reason within two days. One of those was our colleague, James Brigham. We learnt that he too, had Vulci markers in his DNA."

Lisa collapsed, her head in her hands on her lap, sobbing hard.

Mary felt no sympathy. "That wasn't a dream I had last night, was it? You and I were in the Etruscan Hell hearing a plea to an Etruscan God for some curse on you to be lifted. Who were the other two, the man in ancient clothing and the strange woman?"

Lisa took several moments before she spoke. Her voice was weak, as if defeated in combat and she had lost all resistance.

"The man was Larce, a priest of that time," she said. "He had been the priest for the Vulci family and when they asked him to lay a curse on the Tarquinia, he said he couldn't but knew who could. It was his brother, Charun who laid the curse, a priest who had adopted worship of the Underworld Gods."

"And that woman?" Lisa's voice trembled under the shocks she had experienced already that morning.

"She is called Vanth, she is a Goddess of the Underworld, the Angel of Death. She has been making me do all this."

"And that curse, how has it affected you?"

"Charun made the curse so that one person carried the curse at any time, and they would be compelled to kill Tarquinia. The curse lay inside three ornaments, a necklace, a ring and a bracelet. Whoever had those would carry the curse, but only if they were Vulci by descent."

"And you are Vulci and you have them?"

"I do."

"And you are able to identify any Tarquinian descendent, even after more than two thousand years?"

Mary was breathless. What she was hearing was almost beyond belief, it was outside any normal state of the world, she was hearing about old gods, ancient tribal feuds, she had seen two gods, one of those that had ruled the Etruscan civilisation and been worshipped by them, and one of the Underworld. These were mythologies come to life, and she felt she could not take any more such shocks.

"And the sudden deaths of Vulci people? Have you caused those? Do you have a partner in this appalling program you are following?"

Lisa shook her head and gave out another sob.

"That was a second curse, called by the Tarquinian Family as revenge. The demon who placed it said that two Vulci would die for every Tarquinian killed, and the curse could only be placed on a young female before she entered puberty, though it stayed with her afterwards."

Mary looked at Cooper. He was sitting quite motionless, almost catatonic.

Lisa seemed to be recovering, almost as if she had unburdened the dreadful load she had carried for so many years.

"So now you know the whole story, Detective Sergeant Stanton," she said. Her voice was stronger and there was a tone of mockery in it. "And there's still bugger-all you can do about it. You still have no evidence that I killed all those people, much as you are certain that I did, but you can't prove it. And just imagine if you tried using our experience in Hell as evidence in a trial. You'd be thrown out and probably charged with contempt of court."

There was silence in the room for several minutes.

It was Cooper who broke it, by stirring and standing up.

"Mary, we have to go," he said.

Mary understood. Lisa had been correct, they still had no evidence they could use to charge her with multiple murders.

There was no conversation as they drove back to the police station.

Chapter 36 – Passing the Baton

"I can't hold it back," moaned Lisa. "I don't care if that Old God gave me the courage to stop killing, I can't. I need to kill, or I'll go mad."

She was alone in her room, the curtains closed, and she sat on her bed, tears flowing down her cheeks.

"You must, Lisa." The voice of the young girl she had once been rose softly into her mind. "You know that this is the only way to stop this nightmare. You're addicted, and all addicts have terrible trouble breaking free, but you must. Why kill an innocent person to satisfy your addiction? It wouldn't even be a Tarquinian."

"I know," sobbed Lisa. "But this is burning a hole in my gut. If I don't kill again soon, I don't know how bad it will become." She turned and fell on the bed, her face buried in the cover.

"It will get worse and worse, until you go insane," said a new voice. Lisa knew who it was and didn't have to look up.

"I thought the Old God ordered you to leave me alone," she said.

"That old fool?" Vanth's voice was loaded with contempt. "I don't know how he found his way back here, but he's gone back to join all his other obsolete old crocks. He won't get back here again."

Lisa remained silent. She feared that the Angel of Death was correct.

"So you know what you have to do," continued Vanth. "I told you before, plan on returning to Southern Europe, there are hordes of Tarquinia waiting for you to kill."

"Lisa, no! Don't listen to her." The child's voice broke in again. "You must not kill again. If you do, the curse will be back at full strength, and you will be found out sooner or later. Please, stop it now."

"That silly child has become tiresome," said Vanth. "You clearly haven't realised I can hear her as well as you can. It's time she left us."

Lisa felt a sharp pain in her head and the barely heard echo of a child's scream. But she knew her early self had been removed, just how, she didn't understand. She didn't know whether to be grateful or saddened, but she knew the last aid to escaping the nightmare had just died.

She looked up. There was no sign of Vanth. Lisa sat up, stretched, then rose to her feet. The resolve and need to kill again was too strong, she didn't have the strength to resist it, despite what the Old God had promised. And deep inside her, the last trace of her younger self had left her with one fact – this was a way to end the nightmare.

* * *

After three weeks of driving around the country suburbs of her town, Lisa selected her target, a cottage away from other houses by more a kilometre. She knew who lived there, careful observation through binoculars from a distance had revealed that the occupant was a very old man who lived alone. His only visitors were the food delivery truck on Thursdays, a nurse on a Monday morning and a gardener every two weeks. He seemed to have no relatives.

Late one Wednesday evening, Lisa drove up to the front gate, walked the rest of the way and rang the doorbell. After several minutes, she heard footsteps on the wooden floor and the door opened to reveal a curious face. Lisa gave it no chance, she kicked the door open, knocking the old man to the floor, pulled out her boxcutter and sliced his throat wide open. She stood over the old man as he died, watching his astonished, terrified face with enjoyment, relishing the moment when the light died in his eyes. She took a deep breath, sighed with pleasure and returned to her car. She drove the short distance home, feeling at peace with the world. Everything had gone to plan.

* * *

"This makes no sense," said Mary Stanton, seated across from Adrian Cooper. "Cameras recorded her car cruising around that area for three weeks. Frank Carmichael's home security system recorded Lisa walking up the driveway and ringing the bell. It showed clearly how she knocked him down, cut his throat and left. We got a warrant, SOCO found Frank's blood on her shirt and jeans, she'd made no attempt to hide anything. When I went to arrest her with a couple of guys, she almost welcomed me, made no attempt to argue, sat in the patrol car and went to her cell without a word."

"That sure as hell is not the Lisa Kendricks, we've known all these years," said Cooper. "It's almost as if she wanted to be found."

"We've seen this before," said Mary. "Serial killers who seem to think they've fulfilled their dream and gave themselves up, looking forward to being the centre of attention at their trial."

"You think that's it?" Cooper looked doubtful. "That's not like the Lisa we know."

"No, Guv, I don't. From what I remember of that dream that wasn't a dream, there's something else going on. But I'm not going to say anything about that at the trial. That would put an end to my career immediately."

Cooper allowed himself a small smile. "Damn right," he said. "Neither of us is ever going to talk about your meeting with her that day. The world ain't ready to hear about Etruscan Hell, Old Gods and Goddesses of the Underworld. They'll believe in UFOs before that."

"Can I pour you a coffee, Guv?" asked Mary.

* * *

"Members of the Jury, are you agreed on your verdict?"

"We are, My Lord."

"Then in the matter of the murder of Frank Carmichael, how do you find the accused, Lisa Kendricks, guilty or not guilty?"

"Guilty, My Lord."

* * *

Lisa sat on her bed in her cell. She was like that almost every time the guard checked on her through the spy hole. She never spoke, she seemed almost frozen in that position staring at the wall. When her meals were pushed through the slot in the door, she only took the tray half the time and even then, ate half of what was there. When taken outside twice a day for exercise, she never spoke to any other inmates, simply stood against the wall, motionless. If questioned by a guard, she would answer in a dull monotone.

"Why were you so careless?"

Vanth stood against the wall at which Lisa stared all day.

Lisa didn't respond.

"After all those murders successfully hidden over the years, you suddenly leave a trail of clues even a child could follow. Obviously, you will never see the outside of this prison again. Your value to us is gone. But I think that was your intention, you think this will stop the killing. You're wrong, Lisa, the baton will be passed on."

Lisa still said nothing.

"So the contract must be fulfilled. It's time for me to take you to your final destination."

An hour later, the guard looked through the spyhole and saw Lisa slumped on the floor. Quickly, she opened the cell door and bent over the body, checking the pulse on the side of the neck. With a sigh, she went back outside the cell and pressed the emergency button.

Chapter 37 – The Etruscan Hell

Lisa returned to awareness and recognised the gloomy, foreboding surrounds of the Etruscan Hell. She was standing in the middle of what seemed like a vast plain, no ending could be seen in any direction. It made her feel dizzy and she closed her eyes for a moment and then stared down at the ground, rather than face that infinite emptiness.

"Normally, I escort the damned from the place at which they died, by boat to here. I always enjoyed the horror and fear they showed when they realised where they were."

Lisa recognised the voice of Vanth, the Angel of Death. It had been part of her life since the first days of her career of killing people.

"I'm dead, aren't I?" said Lisa.

Vanth let out a short laugh. "Quite correct, Lisa, so you recognise it, because you have been here before, several times in fact, so there was no point in wasting time escorting you here by boat. I took the direct route." The mockery in Vanth's voice was clear. "I wonder how you will cope with a thousand years here."

"A thousand years?" Lisa was horrified. "But the Old God said I would only be here for a hundred years and would not face the tortures."

"That old fool?" Vanth radiated contempt. "I told you before, he and his obsolete old Gods left this world nearly two thousand years ago when our people were evicted from our lands by the Romans. I don't know where they went, nobody cares, and they no longer have a say in what happens in the Underworld. It's the Empire of the Gods of Death, now. I don't know how he got here the last time, but you can be sure, he won't make it again."

Lisa was overwhelmed with fear, and she sank to her knees, sobbing.

"And you think you will avoid the tortures of the damned? Lisa, you killed many innocents, just to satisfy your blood lust and you killed many more merely for the crime of being members of an ancient family. Not one of your victims had ever done you any harm."

Lisa struggled for self-control. "But I never asked to be cursed with something more than two thousand years before I was born. It wasn't my fault."

Vanth laughed again, a cold, frightening sound. "But did you resist? Did you try and stop yourself? No, you didn't. Lisa, you were born a killer, and you embraced your mission with all your heart."

"What happens now?" mumbled Lisa through her sobs.

"This," said Vanth.

A figure appeared a short distance away. It was a man, and as he came nearer, it looked like a dishevelled old tramp, torn, dirty clothing, stained face, but carrying a knife. Lisa recognised him immediately as the first old derelict she had murdered together with the two boys at school. The figure came nearer, came right up to her and plunged the knife into Lisa's chest. She screamed with the pain and clutched at the wound from which blood poured violently.

"This is what you and your little friends did to me," snarled the old man. "I had done nothing to you, you just killed me for the simple fun of it, you and those two boys. Believe me, I'm having my fun now.

The old man repeated the blow, slicing deep into her neck and more blood flowed as the pain doubled and she screamed again. She collapsed to the ground and lay motionless as blood ran all around her.

"How does that feel, Lisa?" said the mocking tones of Vanth. "This is the reverse of what you and your little friends did to that old man. And this is what you will experience every day for the next thousand years. Just think, every morning when you wake up, you cannot look forward to breakfast, sitting in the sun, maybe taking a walk, reading a book. No, none of that is for you. All you can anticipate every day for the next thousand years is to face the horrific pain and anguish as one of your victims takes revenge on you for what you did to them. And no ancient dead God can save you."

Lisa blacked out and would have died, but she was already dead.

Gradually, she came to awareness. There was no sense of having slept or of time passing, but the awful memories of being stabbed to death by a derelict old man with fury in his face were vivid.

She reached for the deep wounds where the knife had cut so hard through her, but there were no signs of injury, nor was there any blood on the ground. She stood up, feeling no pain where the wounds had been.

Full knowledge dawned on her; this would happen again today. The horror of that filled her body and she trembled violently. She could do nothing. The vast plain without end showed no signs of anything else in her world. Slowly, she walked around, hoping to see some physical sign that there was something else in the emptiness.

And then there was.

A tall, slender man stood before her. He carried a bayonet from a military rifle, and he stared at her coldly. She recognised him at once. Major General Adams looked as military as his title and career suggested and as she had seen him when he visited her school.

"You and your friends killed me because I had descended more than two thousand years from an ancient, honoured family, the Tarquinia. None of that line had harmed you, but you killed me anyway. Now I reclaim the honour of returning the action."

Lisa screamed as the General raised the bayonet and struck down at Lisa's shoulder. The pain was horrific, the weapon was heavy, wide and pierced deep down into her body as blood erupted into her face and neck. The old man pulled the blade out, then swung an underhand blow into her stomach, repeating the dreadful agony of the first blow and resulting in a similar torrent of blood down her front and onto the ground.

"I can't bear it," was the only coherent thought in her mind as she sank to the ground, pain enveloping her entire body. Dimly, she was aware of the General standing close to her, blood dripping from the weapon in his hand.

"We of the Tarquinia will watch every one of your deaths," he said. "And do you not know, that for every one of us you murdered, two of the Vulci tribe died within two days? No, of course you do not, how could you? So every time you die at the hands of your victims, remember that your entire mission of killing us only resulted in more of your own family dying."

Even through the pain and the horror as the light died, Lisa could still feel the terrible sensation that everything she had done had only caused worse to her own family of the Vulci.

For the second time, Lisa died a death that wasn't a death.

As she returned to consciousness, she saw a young man sitting a short distance away. She struggled to understand what was happening, though that was almost impossible in the horror of recalling where she was and what had happened.

"Remember me?" asked the young man. "I was hitchhiking in Europe, and you picked me up in your campervan."

Now Lisa remembered and she shivered, knowing what was about to happen.

"You led me into the bushes and then stabbed me as we were making love. You are one evil woman, Lisa and I'm going to enjoy this next step." He stood up and walked nearer to Lisa who remained lying prone. He kicked her onto her back, pulled a knife from a scabbard on his belt and thrust it into her belly. Again, Lisa screamed with the unbearable agony of the deep cut.

"Is this fun, Lisa? Did you enjoy as much as you did when you killed me while we were fucking? Does this give you the same thrill? You never even knew my name when you killed me. Now I'm just going to watch while you die."

He stood upright, just a short distance from her. Her last memories before the blackness descended was of the man smiling as he looked down on her at his feet, blood pouring all over the ground and onto his shoes.

The undeath enveloped her once more.

There was a difference when she awoke again. Struggling through the deep horror and fear of what would face her this time, she saw three people waiting for her.

"Lisa, I know you didn't kill me, but you set your two boys onto me, didn't you?"

"Jake!" she exclaimed, remembering how she had watched Pete and Dylan garotte her boyfriend with the device she had made. Then she recognised the other two figures. Pete and Dylan stood silently, watching her.

"You killed us both," said Dylan. "After we had helped you kill others, and after we had killed Jake, then you turned on us."

"But how can you be here, you and the others? Did they have to be sent to Hell to torture me?

Pete smiled. "But we're not here, Lisa. All the people you remember as victims, they're not, we're demons taking on the image so that we can make the torture worse."

The two boys suddenly moved and seized her arms, turning her so that her back was before Jake. She saw the garotte curve over her head and down to her neck where it tightened as Jake pulled hard. The pain was dreadful, a sharp line on her throat, stifling her breathing and then cutting deep into the flesh, slicing into her breathing and sending blood flowing down her front. She couldn't breathe, she could only look at the faces of Pete and Dylan as they watched her with broad smiles on their faces.

She blacked out into her temporary death, but it seemed she returned to consciousness immediately. He throat was whole again, she gasped furiously for breath and succeeded. But the improvement was temporary.

"Our turn," said Dylan and Pete together and simultaneously slashed at her throat with razor-sharp box cutters. The breathing horror was repeated. She had time for only one thought as she died again. "God, please help me," she thought as the darkness descended once more.

This time, she woke to see Vanth standing above her.

"Are you enjoying this, Lisa?" said the Angel of Death. "Are you getting the same erotic thrill you got when you murdered these people?"

Lisa struggled to speak through the remembered pain and fear.

"Please, God of the Etruscans, you promised me this wouldn't happen," she whispered. "Please, stop it."

Vanth laughed in huge contempt.

"I've already told you, silly girl, those obsolete old farts have vanished, all of them, they've gone into the mists of ancient history. Nobody will save you, you've only had three days of the thousand years in front of you. And every day will be same as you've already had. Just think of that, Lisa, dying in terrible pain, every day for a thousand years."

Lisa struggled to her feet and stared at the Angel of Death. She felt some courage, some strength returned to her, slightly suppressing the fear, the horror and the memory of unbearable pain.

"Gods don't die," she said, her voice rasping from the shocks of the last three days. "The True Gods may be somewhere else, but I have no doubts they are well aware of what you are doing and how you disobeyed their orders."

Staring at Vanth, Lisa saw the Demon's face change, from the smiling contempt to utter horror and fear, as if she was echoing Lisa's experience.

"That is correct," boomed a massive voice from nowhere and everywhere. "This was not what I ordered, Vanth. It is time for this to end."

Vanth fell to her knees, covering her face. "I am sorry, my lord," she sobbed. "I was fulfilling my role as the Goddess of the Underworld."

"You and your fellow Underworld Gods were merely fulfilling the same bloodlust and sadism you have always followed. This is now at an end. Vanth, you and your gods will come with me for your own reckoning."

The voice softened in tone and reduced in volume.

"Lisa," said a pleasant baritone voice. "All this is over. This entire curse is well past its due date. You can return to the usual experience of a dead human, the curse is gone, you can start again, but something of what you have gone through will carry on to the next stage."

Badly wanting to ask what the next stage was, Lisa just barely heard a frantic scream from Vanth as the vast plain vanished and Lisa again blacked out, but without the dreadful pain that had caused it on the previous occasions.

* * *

"You have a beautiful, healthy little girl," said the maternity ward nurse, holding the tiny bundle. "Would you like to hold her?"

"You're sure she's okay?" The woman sitting upright in the bed reached out and took hold of the new baby. "Oh my, Rick, just look at her. She's perfect."

The man by her side wiped away a few tears and leaned over to look at the child.

"She sure is," he said and gently kissed the forehead of his new daughter.

"Have you decided what you'll call her?" asked the nurse, smiling at the evident joy in the couple.

"We've always known," said the mother. "She's called Lisa."

"Yes, somehow we knew from the moment we learnt that Margaret was pregnant, we'd call her Lisa," said Rick. "It was almost as if she was telling us herself."

"That's wonderful," said the nurse. "I'll leave you now to enjoy being parents."

Chapter 38 - The Baton is Passed

"Philip, at last we're home, and we have our little baby!" Norma Baird turned in her seat to look back at the cot securely strapped into the back seat of the car as her husband switched off the engine and climbed out. He opened the back door and waited for Norma to come round, and together, they lifted the cot out of the car and carried it into their modest house in the Birmingham suburb of Acocks Green.

"Isn't she just adorable?" proclaimed Norma. "We were so lucky that we were able to adopt this little girl. I feel awfully sorry that her mother couldn't manage it, but it proved lucky for us. Let's just hold her for a while."

She picked up the tiny bundle and cradled it, looking down with a smile.

"My turn," said Philip after a few minutes and repeated Norma's actions. "Let's get her into her cot," he said finally, and they put the child into the cot they had set up in their bedroom.

"She's beautiful," said Norma. "Philip, we're going to be such a wonderful family. I feel terribly sad that her mother, Lisa was unable to keep her, but it makes us so happy."

"Let's have a drink to that," said Philip.

Two Years Later

"I dunno, Norma, I just don't seem to be able to get through to Zoe. She just ignores me, doesn't want me to hold her and won't play at all." Philip looked down at the little girl sitting silently in her seat. Her face was angry, though she stayed silent.

"Same with me. She lets me feed and clean her, but I've never got a smile of any sort from her. She doesn't play with her toys, not even the beautiful doll I bought her. And she ignores anyone who comes round, even my nieces who really want to play with her."

"It's not what we expected. Two-year-olds should be running around, being noisy, wanting to play all the time. She just sits there." Philip looked sad, almost ready to weep. "Our little girl isn't giving us any joy at all."

"The doctor can't understand it," said Norma. "There's nothing wrong with her, he said, but he's never encountered this sort of anti-social behaviour in such a young child."

Fourteen Months Later

"That was horrible," said Norma. "We both thought that getting a kitten would draw her out a bit, all kids are supposed to love kittens and puppies."

"We sure goofed there," agreed Norma. "She just started kicking the poor little animal. I had to rescue it and put Zoe in her room, she was screaming so loud. I'm glad Jessie down the road was happy to take it. God almighty, what have we got here? We were so looking forward to being a family." She burst into tears and ran into the bedroom.

"That sure as hell was the biggest mistake of our

lives," muttered Philip. "I wonder what her mother was like? I wondered why she refused to even see the kid when she was born, let us take it as soon as we could. Maybe she knew what she was going to be like, but how can any mother know that when she was just born?"

Thirty Months Later

"We're not throwing a birthday party for her, are we?" said Philip, fully aware of what the answer would be.

"How the hell could we?" replied Norma. "Who would come? None of the kids in the street will come near the house anymore and nobody from school will, either. She's got no friends there, it seems. The Principal is really worried. She said Zoe causes problems for everybody. She suggested we have her put in a special needs sort of school."

"I asked her if she wanted a party, and she just snarled. I've never heard a child actually snarl before." The distress on Philip's face was obvious. "God, she's six years old, and she's never had a friend, never read a book, never watched a television program, just sits in her room. What the hell does she do in there all evening?"

Norma shook her head, tears flowing down her cheeks. She walked up to Philip, and they clung together, seeking comfort from their closeness.

"I think she goes out at night after we've gone to bed," she said.

"You're right," replied Philip. "I'm pretty sure I hear her come in about three in the morning, it's just when I wake up as I do almost every night."

"I don't even want to think about what she does out there," said Norma. "She's six, what in God's name is a six-year-old doing, wandering about on her own in the middle of the night?"

One Month Later

The Birmingham Standard

Police are still baffled by the outbreak of killings of cats and dogs around Acocks Green and nearby suburbs. So far, seven dogs and six cats have been found early in the morning over the last six weeks, all of them with their throats cut with a sharp blade. Police are assuming a single perpetrator, but the motive is unknown. The pets' owners are understandably distraught, wondering who could be so cruel and vicious as to kill innocent animals.

Police are offering a thousand pound reward for any information leading to the arrest of the culprit.

Six Years Later

"Good morning," said the tall, handsome man in the well-cut suit standing at the doorway after Norma had answered the doorbell. "I'm a lawyer, acting for the estate of Lisa Kendricks."

"Lisa ..? That's Zoe's mother, right?" Norma could

not hide her shock. Despite the appearance of the man, Norma felt a twinge of fear at the sight. There was something about him..

"She was, Mrs Baird, that's correct. But she died a year after Zoe's birth. Can I come in and tell you what this is about?"

Stunned into silence, Norma stood back and allowed the visitor to enter, feeling a slight shiver as he passed her. She led him to the lounge where Philip was reading the newspaper. Norma found her voice.

"Philip, there's a lawyer with something about Lisa Kendrick's estate."

"What?" Philip stood up, folded the newspaper and stared at the newcomer.

"My name is Gerald Hawkins. As I told your wife, Mr Baird, I'm a lawyer representing the estate of Zoe's late mother, Lisa Kendricks." He handed over a card to Philip, who studied it carefully.

"Take a seat, Mr Hawkins," said Philip. Norma could see the same uncertainty in her husband as she was feeling. Something was wrong with this visitor. All three took seats, Philip and Norma on the couch, holding hands for security, the lawyer in one of the armchairs, taking a wad of papers from his breast pocket as he sat down, placing his briefcase by his side.

"My arrangement with Lisa was a private one over some years," continued the newcomer. "You will soon get a call from the executor of her estate, as per the terms of her will, which states that at twelve, Zoe should be advised of her mother's life following Zoe's adoption. But I can tell you what it's all about."

He smiled and referred to the papers in his hand.

"You won't know about this, because the story was sharply suppressed, but shortly after Zoe's birth, Lisa was convicted of a rather savage murder of an old man in his house."

"Murder? Lisa killed somebody Why would she do anything like that?" Philip was shaken, sitting half upright. Norma simply gasped loudly.

"There was never any motive identified," said Hawkins. "It appeared to be entirely without cause, simply an act of senseless savagery."

"Good God," exclaimed Philip and sat back in his seat. He and Norma looked at each other and the unspoken communication was clear. There was something terribly wrong about this meeting and what it was telling them about their adopted daughter.

"Strangely, she left plenty of clues and the police arrested her within two days of the murder," continued Hawkins. "But she died in prison three weeks after her arrest and sentencing. There was absolutely nothing to explain her death, she was in good health, though her appearance was of a much older woman than her actual thirty-six."

"This is dreadful," muttered Norma.

"Anyway, what I have come about is rather better news," said Hawkins. "Lisa had made a will after the birth of Zoe. You won't know this, but Lisa was a very rich woman, having inherited the entire estate of her parents who had died when Lisa was just a year or two more than Zoe is now."

"We knew nothing of this," said Philip. "Part of the adoption agreement was that we would not know more than Lisa's name and age. We found it all very strange, particularly as she didn't want to meet us or even see Zoe when she was born."

"How much as we talking here?" asked Norma.

Hawkins looked down at the papers. "There is cash held in trust until Zoe is eighteen, at which point it is passed to her," he said. "The total of that is one million, eight hundred thousand pounds."

"One million..?" Norma looked stunned.

"And then there is the house," continued Hawkins. "That has been managed by a real estate company since Lisa's incarceration and is has been rented at excellent rates ever since. That income has been added to the proceeds of selling the house. However, the last tenants went overseas two months ago, and the house was sold, bringing in something over five hundred thousand pounds. The terms of the will state that the proceeds from the sale of the house be passed directly to Zoe's adoptive parents, that is you, Mr and Mrs Baird."

There was a moment of silence from the couch.

"Five hundred thousand..?" Norma was almost breathless.

"The executor will confirm that when he calls in the next few days," said Hawkins. "And now I have just one more thing to settle." He reached into his briefcase and brought out a wooden box the size of a hardback book. "This is from my personal relationship with Lisa. She didn't want the executor to know about it, and I am now following her private instructions." He opened the box and displayed the contents to the couple.

They leaned forward and stared at them.

"Is that gold?" asked Norma, her voice trembling.

"It is, indeed," said Hawkins. "So is the ring with a gigantic precious stone. Both are worth a great deal of money, as much because of their historic connections. The bracelet is simply copper but also has enormous value because of its provenance."

"Please explain," said Philip.

"Again, you won't know this, but Lisa's father was an internationally renowned expert on the Etruscan civilisation that once ruled large parts of Europe until dispersed by the Romans. He took these items from an Etruscan tomb, quite illegally, and gave them to Lisa. That gold necklace alone is worth over a hundred thousand pounds."

"But we'd have these illegally," said Philip. "We should just report this to the police."

"You won't do that," said Hawkins. "What you *will* do is give them to Zoe immediately for her to do as she wishes. And I promise you, if you even mention them outside yourselves, that money from the sale of the house will be confiscated and given to charity. Lisa was most determined that Zoe would have them."

Philip and Norma were both breathing hard. They looked at each other and came to an agreement.

"We will give them to Zoe," said Norma. "But I just don't understand any of this."

"Your understanding is unnecessary," said Hawkins. "Your compliance is, however."

All pleasantness had vanished to be replaced by obvious menace. Philip recognised it and got to his feet.

"Time you left, Mr Hawkins," he said.

"Agreed," said the visitor and made his own way out of the house.

"What an appalling man," said Norma.

"Damn right. Let's check on him."

He took the business card he'd been given and went to the computer on the desk. He keyed in the call for a search engine and entered the lawyer's name.

"No entry matches this entry," said the line on the screen.

"I bet the phone number gives the same result," muttered Philip and took out his mobile phone. A moment later, he looked up at Norma. "He doesn't exist," he said. "What the hell is going on?"

Three days later, the mystery deepened.

"Mr Baird, my name is Andrew Hurd, a solicitor with Hollier and Company."

"Yes, Mr Hurd, you are calling about the estate of Lia Kendricks?"

"I am, but I must ask you, how did you know? Nobody outside the firm knows about that."

"I'll explain later. Why are you calling?"

"We are the executors of Lisa Kendricks' will. We will need you to come to our Birmingham office to discuss the final details. Can you give me a convenient date?"

"You're going to tell me about the one million, eight hundred-thousand-pound inheritance for Zoe and the half million from the sale of the house."

The gasp of shock from the man on the phone was distinct.

"Mr Baird, how could you possibly know that? The will has been locked away in our files for twelve years."

"That lawyer, Gerald Hawkins came and told us."

"We know nobody of that name. This is beyond comprehension. Can you come to our office as soon as possible to discuss this? It's critical."

"Tomorrow okay? Say nine in the morning?"

"We'll see you then."

"Zoe, a man came by, he asked us to give you this. It's a present from your mother."

"My mother? What the hell has she got to give me?"

"Why don't you have a look?" Norma handed the box over. Zoe took it without expression, opened it and studied the contents. She seemed to freeze into immobility.

"The man who gave us this was very firm," said Norma. "He said you must not talk about this to anyone. Do you understand any of this?"

Zoe looked up. "All of it," she said. "Will you leave me, please?"

Norma left her daughter's room with a mix of sadness and confusion.

That evening, Zoe sat before the mirror on the dressing table in her bedroom and opened the box. She felt a strange warmth run through her body as she touched each of the ornaments in turn, then took up the gold necklace. She put it around her neck and studied the image in the mirror as the sense of warmth grew stronger. She decided it looked wonderful.

With the strange warmth came strange images. She saw bodies of people lying in pools of blood, but while such images would have been disturbing, they weren't. Instead, they gave her sensations of great pleasure. For a few moments, she enjoyed those sensations, then moved onto the next stage.

She picked up the huge ring. It was far too large to fit on any finger, but she slipped it on the ring finger of her left hand and clutched it firmly.

The pleasing images remained, but the pleasurable sensations were replaced by waves of anger. She had no idea of why, or what was causing the anger, but sensed the relationship between that and the images of bleeding corpses from earlier. She felt a desperate need to cause more of those corpses, the desire to kill. Her hands itched to hold a murderous, lethal knife and plunge it into a living, human body.

With those urges, she remembered how she had killed dogs and cats during her evening adventures just a few years before. The pleasure she had experienced slicing into the bodies of the animals and watching them die in pools of blood and great distress was a shadow of what she felt she needed to do now.

Breathing hard with excitement, she slipped the copper bracelet onto her right wrist.

To her astonishment, her image in the mirror had changed, looking more like an adult woman, but still obviously her. And the heat in her body had risen. Something else happened in her mind. Now she knew who the objects of her new-found killing urge should be

"So that's what I have to do," she whispered with a surge of delight.

** The End **